Z: THE LOST CITY

BY P.K. HAWKINS

SEVEREDPRESS

Z: THE LOST CITY

WWW.SEVEREDPRESS.COM

ISBN: 978-1-923165-15-1

CHAPTER ONE

For a man who used to make his living adventuring in the far corners of the world, Jonas Drammond had most definitely seen better days. Or at least that was what his few remaining friends told him. He himself barely looked in a mirror anymore, unless one counted occasionally seeing his reflection in a bottle of booze. But as much as he couldn't get himself to care too much about what he looked like anymore, he still found himself straightening his hair as the little icon on his computer said it was connecting him to his telepresence meeting. He wasn't so far gone that he didn't realize he needed to at least try putting his best foot forward if he wanted to find some way to keep the lights on and a roof over his head in the increasing shabbiness of the apartment around him.

He made one last check to make sure there wasn't anything embarrassing in view behind him, and scrabbled to hide the two empty whiskey bottles he found sitting knocked over in plain view on a bookshelf. He was sure that most people who would contact him would have known by now that he'd spent the last several years crawled into a bottle, but just in case this woman wasn't aware of that, he didn't exactly want to volunteer the information.

Jonas wasn't in the habit of accepting random Zoom calls for job offers from people he barely knew, but he'd asked a few contacts who would still talk to him, and they said this woman was legitimate. She was some sort of well-known researcher at a university in Brazil, and apparently she had money and reasons to hire guides all the time. Jonas didn't know why someone like that would be looking for him, then, a washed-up former adventurer that hadn't been anywhere near her country for going on five years now, but he certainly couldn't afford to blow her off. Not if he wanted to entertain any notion at all of one day regaining just an ounce of his dignity.

The call on his laptop connected, and he found himself staring at a beautiful young woman somewhere in her thirties, probably a good ten or fifteen years younger than him. The view behind her was of some spacious office with books and art objects all over, sometimes in neat cases and other times in haphazard piles. She spoke with a Brazilian accent, but not one as heavy as he would have expected. “Hello. Mr. Drammond?”

“Hi. Yes. I assume that you must be Miss Efigenia Araujo.”

“That is correct,” she said. She paused as she looked at him with an assessing glare. She didn’t give away any of her thoughts with her expression, but Jonas was sure he looked less than impressive. He’d put on the cleanest, least stain-covered shirt he had for this call, but that wasn’t saying much, and his face was overgrown with an unruly, graying beard that probably made him look a little like a crazed hermit. At least he was sober so far today, and he did the best he could to look like he wasn’t as far gone as he felt.

“I’m extremely grateful that you’re willing to take this meeting,” Efigenia said. “It took me quite some time to track you down, and I’m starting to get a little worried as I’m in a time crunch.”

“Yes, well, I’ve been out of the game for a while, so I’m just grateful that you thought of me. I do have to wonder, though, why you seemed so keen on finding me specifically. Got to be honest here, at this point I would think you could do better than me."

"Well, I have a very specific problem, and I think you may be the only person in the entire world who can help me."

Jonas sat up a little straighter. This wasn't the first time he'd heard a similar sentiment. It was, however, the first time in the five years since the disaster, as he called it. Everyone in his field knew about it, and likely everyone that would possibly be interested in hiring him. So if this woman still thought he would be important even after finding out his history, then he had to take notice.

"I can certainly make myself of service to you, but I do need to know a little more about what it is you're looking for from me before I can say whether or not I can provide it."

"Well, before I say anything about that, can you tell me a little bit about what happened with Arlene Carter?"

Jonas tensed. He knew this question was going to come up, but he hadn't expected it to happen so quickly. "I'm sure that you've done your homework on me, so then you already know everything I've told anyone else."

"Yes, I've read the various reports, but I'm not bringing it up just to test you or make you uncomfortable. I think there might be something in your story that will have direct bearing on everything I'm about to tell you."

While that made sense, Jonas had to suppress the urge to immediately press the end button on the video call and immediately find the closest open bottle of booze. He'd relived all of this many, many times before, but it never got any easier. Five years on, and he still had horrific dreams.

"Fine. What you probably already know is that a woman named Arlene Carter hired me to lead her and a group of four other people into the far western regions of the Amazonas region of Brazil. While I knew of her before that and knew that she was an archeologist, she never told me what exactly she was hoping to find. She just showed me some general areas on the map she wanted to go to. That wasn't my usual way of working, and I was suspicious from the beginning, but I vetted her with some other guides I knew and they said she was okay. She was also paying far higher than my normal fee, so I was willing to avoid asking questions. We were out in the rainforest for just about a week when she and everyone else in the group but me mysteriously disappeared."

Efigenia cocked her head and frowned. "I'm going to need more information about when and how the disappearance happened."

Jonas sighed. Going over all this was painful, but he didn't see any way to avoid talking about it. "We made camp for the night. I slept, and when I woke up all five of them were gone along with about half of their equipment. The rest was just left behind like they intended to come back. I tried to track them, but to my dismay they seemed to be able to cover their tracks, like they very intentionally didn't want me to see where they were headed. I searched for them for three days before I was forced to go back to civilization and report them missing. It destroyed my reputation as a guide, but I'm sure you already know that."

"I do, but I have reason to believe there might be a little more to their disappearance than the gross negligence that you've been accused of. I don't think their vanishing is your fault at all."

Jonas took a deep breath. He'd talked with a lot of people and colleagues in the five years since he had lost every single person he was guiding on his final trip into the Amazon Rainforest, and the impression that he'd usually gotten, whether the people would say it out loud or not, was that only the most incompetent person could possibly have let this happen. The fact that Jonas had been considered one of the best in the business for years prior to this didn't matter after only one major incident. So to hear someone else - a potential client, no less – say they didn't think it was his fault was a great relief.

"But there was a specific detail I found in your account that I thought might be more important than anyone is giving you credit for," Efigenia said.

"And what's that?"

"In your original missing persons report you filed, there was something that you didn't seem to mention much of elsewhere. You said that on the second day of looking for them, you came across a sheer rock face, maybe six or seven feet high, that stretched for some distance. You followed it for a while before seeing something that led you to believe that perhaps they had gone in a different direction. Do you remember that?"

"Um, yeah, I do, but I don't know what that has to do with anything."

"Whether or not it has anything to do with their disappearance remains to be seen," she said. "But I think it has absolutely everything to do with something I'm looking for. You see, I did a little digging into what we believe the geology of that area should be, and a flat stretch of rock for that distance doesn't match something that should have been formed naturally in that area."

Jonas took a long pause before asking his next question. "Miss Araujo, maybe you should tell me exactly what it is you're expecting me to do for you and why."

"I can certainly do that, but first I've got to ask you if you know a little bit about history. Tell me, have you ever heard of an explorer named Percy Harrison Fawcett?"

Jonas paused for a moment and thought about it. "The name is familiar. I've definitely heard it before, but I couldn't tell you anything about him."

"Fawcett was a British cartographer and artillery officer. The British Army would often send him to places that Britain wanted to explore or take over, so he could survey the place and prepare the rest of their explorers or troops. He made several visits to the region on their behalf, and he would often make claims about things that he'd seen that no one else would believe, like the time he claimed he shot a sixty-foot anaconda. By

1914 he had started to believe there was a large lost city he called Z somewhere in the Matto Grosso region of the Amazon forest. He also found a document that came to be known as Manuscript 512, which is currently housed in my department at the University of Rio de Janeiro. It was written by some unknown person claiming to have found a city full of arches, statues, and hieroglyphs in the year 1753. Fawcett made a couple of attempts to find the city, including one in 1925 with his son Jack. But they all disappeared on that last expedition, and were believed to have died in their quest."

Jonas listened to all this intently, but there was one specific detail that caught his notice. "The Matto Grosso region is nearly all the way across the country from where I was when I lost Carter and her team, the eastern side instead of the western side. So I'm not quite sure yet what the connection is."

"Very good observation," she said. "I'll get to that point in just a second. There were others after Fawcett who went looking for the city, and the way these stories usually go, you would expect that it had never been found. Except most archeologists believe that it *has* been found. In

1925, soon after Fawcett's expedition disappeared, westerners found an archeological site called Kuhikugu, which was found at the headwaters of the Xingu River. While not exactly the magnificent city that Fawcett would have expected, it contained the ruins of roughly twenty towns that could have held up to fifty thousand people. Everyone assumed that Manuscript 512 had just been full of exaggerations about Kuhikugu, and for the most part people stopped searching for Z."

"Are you saying that you think everyone got it wrong about this Kuhikugu and Z being the same place?" Jonas asked.

"I think so, because I have found something very interesting. Because deep within our university's archives, I found another manuscript, one that I believe was written by someone responding to the writer of Manuscript 512. In it, it clarifies a number of details that were left vague, and these new details suggest to me that Fawcett and everyone else was looking for the Lost City of Z in entirely the wrong portion of Brazil. This new manuscript suggests the city was actually on the far western side of the country, somewhere in the rainforest north of what is now modern-day Porto Velho and Rio Branco. Is this starting to sound familiar to you?"

It most certainly was, and Jonas found himself sitting at rigid attention in his seat. "Rio Branco was the staging point I used with Carter and her team for her expedition."

Efigenia nodded. "I found something else very interesting regarding this new manuscript. The university keeps a record of visitors to its archives, and this particular manuscript has only been viewed by one outside visitor in the last ten years. Do you care to guess who that visitor was?"

It was an easy guess. "It was Arlene Carter, wasn't it?"

"Correct. She visited the archives three times in the year prior to her disappearance, with the last visit being only a week before your expedition with her. Mr. Drammond, I think that the reason Carter was out there was that she was looking for the Lost City of Z, and for some reason she wanted to keep what little she knew a secret. And more than that, I think you might have actually been there and not known it."

"The geological oddity you were talking about," Jonas said. "You don't think it was a natural rock formation at all."

"I don't. I think you were right outside the City of Z and didn't even realize it."

The next words were out of Jonas's mouth before he even had time to consider whether they were wise. "Whatever you're planning on doing, I'm in. When do we leave?"

CHAPTER TWO

Jonas was used to expeditions taking a lot of time to plan, so he was shocked when he realized Professor Araujo needed him in Brazil within a matter of days, if possible. Thankfully, even through the alcohol-induced haze of the last four or five years, he had kept his passport up to date, so with her help planning his flights he was able to make it down to Brazil from his home in the United States rather quickly. She said that they were running up against a clock, but she hadn't taken a lot of time to explain to him what that meant. It seemed unlikely to him that a lost city sitting hidden in the Amazon for who knew how long was in any danger of disappearing if they didn't find it immediately, but Efigenia was reluctant to give him many details over Zoom. That lack of transparency bothered him a little, given that his lack of information on his previous expedition had likely added to his inability to find the others once they had been lost, but she had assured him that it was all above board and that there would be plenty of time to explain once she picked him up at the airport. This would not be a situation like last time when things were kept from him, she said. He was skeptical, but the money and situation were too good to let that stop him.

He took a normal commercial flight down to Manaus, then from there got on a small single engine plane that took him to a small private airfield outside of Porto Velho. He was the only one on the plane, so when someone was waiting as he got off, there was no doubt that she was there for him.

Efigenia Araujo looked like a completely different person under the clear Brazilian sky than she had as a six inch by six-inch image on Jonas's computer. Part of that was probably because of the dim lighting in her tiny office, but mostly, Jonas thought, there was simply a presence to her that didn't fully come out unless she was out in the open. She was tall and held herself like a statue as she stood waiting for him outside the car. And while she wasn't wearing makeup, she had the kind of face that still looked like some subtle color had been added to it anyway.

She saw him right away, and took his hand to

shake as he approached her. “Jonas, it’s great to finally meet you in person.” He saw the way her eyes scanned him up and down, taking in the changes since she had last seen him. The most notable difference would be the near-lack of facial hair, but he was wearing new clothes and had new luggage, although he had known better than to go into the field with brand new boots. Honestly, the all-new clothes might not be the best for the reputation of someone who was supposed to make his living leading people through the inhospitable places of Earth, but he was just happy to feel new and clean again. He’d almost forgotten what it felt like.

“I’m happy to be here,” Jonas said.

“I want to get started as quickly as possible, but if you wanted to go to my hotel first for a rest, that could…”

“I can sleep tonight when we’re in the field, if you already have everything we need to get started. Although…”

“It’s all in the car, but if you wanted to check all the equipment first to make sure there isn’t anything else you think you might need, that would be appreciated.”

He did exactly that, doing a detailed inventory

of her equipment in the parking lot, expecting something to be missing that would delay the start of their journey. However, she had included everything they would need, yet still kept it all compact and economic. There was an efficiency to her packing that told him a lot about her character, and also that she was someone who knew her way around working in the field. This was not a woman who only spent her time in the office.

"This is really something I should have asked earlier, but this is something you've done before, isn't it?" he asked. "I found some evidence that you've done field work, but it looks like you may be fairly experienced."

"I'm not just a researcher from my cozy little place at the university," Efigenia said. "I've done plenty of field work, including lots of time spent at Kuhikugu. That's how I started to suspect that it wasn't really the so-called Lost City of Z. While I may not be anywhere near as experienced as someone like you in wilderness survival, I at least have the basics I need to survive and the resources to get me everything we need to start out immediately."

"Are you going to be able to fill me in on why

it was so important that we do this now rather than take time to set up a full expedition?" Jonas asked. "While a trip with just the two us may be faster, it has its potential hazards."

"Get in," Efigenia said. "I'll fill you in on the way."

The car was a four-wheel drive, but he knew it wouldn't be able to take them that far into their journey. There would be a few dirt roads that got them slightly into the interior of the rainforest, but they only had less than an hour of driving before they would have to start out on foot, followed by at most two days of walking through the rainforest before they would be close to where he had lost his previous expedition. Once the driving started, Efigenia wasted no time explaining exactly what was going on.

"Mr. Drammond, are you familiar with a corporation called Graft-Horton?"

"I've heard of it. I know it was created by men named Julian Horton and Cristof Graft. I think Horton's been dead for a while now, right? Graft gets a lot of press, but more for his political influence than for whatever it is that his company does."

"The company has its hands in a lot of things,

from fossil fuels to tech funding, but what is relevant to us is their land and development work. During the previous political regime here in Brazil, Graft-Horton was able to buy up large portions of land that normally wouldn't have been up for sale. While the current politicians publicly condemn the company's land-grabbing, behind closed doors they still work with Graft-Horton and let them develop land that they haven't even bought at all. They've been bulldozing certain portions of the forest to build investment properties for rich outsiders who never even set foot in the country."

"While I understand the direction you're probably going with this, I have to say I would find it a little hard to believe that they would be developing anything yet in the regions where I was last leading expeditions," Jonas said. "The place where Carter's team disappeared was very deep into the forest. It would be years of work before any major developments could be done in that region."

"That doesn't change that Graft-Horton is still planning on claiming huge portions of that region for their own. Legally they don't yet have any claim on most of it, but there are reports of them already clearing large swaths at the edges of the forest. The reason it is so urgent that we find the Lost City of Z now is that, for the time being, it's still now private land. If Graft-Horton were able to sufficiently surround the area before the city is found, then outside groups like us will lose all ability and legal right to even go in there."

"So what exactly are you hoping to accomplish to prevent that?"

"I have some contacts with the United Nations Educational, Scientific and Cultural Organization," Efigenia said.

Jonas nodded. He was familiar with UNESCO. They were responsible for keeping various ancient and cultural sites safe throughout the world. He had even led expeditions to quite a few of those sites during his many years as a guide.

"Normally, it takes a long time for a site to be considered for inclusion in the registry of UNESCO World Heritage Sites, but if I can come back with proof that the Lost City of Z exists before Graft-Horton cuts off all ability for outside forces to reach it, my contact can guarantee that they'll be able to provide protection from the company. It won't be easy for them, and there will have to be a lot of lawyers involved, but it will be harder for Graft-Horton to go against the UN than it would be for them to go against a bunch of random activists trying to preserve the region by tying themselves to bulldozers."

"I suppose this is probably a stupid question, but I have to ask just so all the bases are covered: have you considered just going to Graft-Horton and telling them what you think is there? Maybe offer them some kind of stake in keeping the site safe if it exists?"

Efigenia shook her head. "I did look into it just to see if there was any possibility of that, but Graft-Horton has been using some very sketchy and occasionally disturbing tactics to get the land they want for their developments. There are even rumors that they might have had a hand in the assassination of a local advocate for the rights of the indigenous tribes of the area. That's not anything anyone can prove, of course, but it is very clear at this point that they would have zero interest in even keeping the site in existence as a tourist destination for them to exploit. They see more money in the land as real estate investments, and nothing is going to get them to change their minds short of very powerful people being on our side to stop them. And in order to get those powerful people on our side, we first have to prove that the site even exists."

"Still, though, it doesn't feel like we had to start out on the expedition immediately. Even with all you said, there's no way Graft-Horton would be able to completely block off this entire region to explorers, at least not just yet," Jonas said. "Is there something else you aren't telling me?"

Efigenia didn't say anything for a very long moment, then answered. "I didn't exactly want to say anything, because it's possible that someone within the company is trying to play me. But I have a contact within Graft-Horton, someone well-placed, and they warned me that another expedition is planning on going into the area, one funded directly by the company. And their plan, if they find Z, is to blow it up."

Jonas had to blink and wonder if he had heard that correctly. "I'm sorry, what?"

"Yes, I know it sounds ridiculous. You'd think there's no way anyone would actually try to do that. And that's why I almost think that someone is trying to pull a prank on me or trick me into doing something that would discredit me or my theory about the lost city. But my contact says this expedition is heading into the Amazon today, and that they have most of the same information that I do about the likely location of Z, and that the company plans on destroying the site so that it isn't even possible for it to be discovered by anyone else before Graft-Horton can make their move on the land. That's why we have to move now, and why our expedition needs to be small, so we can beat them there."

"Well, who is this contact?" Jonas asked. "Is he or she trustworthy?"

"That's just the problem. I don't know. All the tips I've been getting have been completely anonymous with no way for me to verify anything. For all I know, it's a trick to get me to find the location for them, and they're just following us and getting ready to knock us off as soon as we get there."

"Knock us off?" Jonas asked. "You honestly think they might try to kill you?"

"Graft-Horton has been suspected of far worse in the past, but no one has ever been able to prove it. Mysterious deaths just seem to have a way of happening to people working against them."

Both of them stopped to stare at each other for a second, then looked back into the rearview mirrors to see if there were any cars following them. But they were well away from the main roads at this point, and there was absolutely no sign that they were being followed.

"Well that's a cheery thought," Jonas said. "It's also the kind of thing that you probably should have told me before I came down here."

"Would it have made a difference?"

Jonas had to take a pause to think about that. In truth, he hadn't stopped to think about any of this much since he had first received Efigenia's initial email. Going back to civilization without Carter and the rest of her team had been the worst moment of his entire life, both for the embarrassment and the knowledge that doing so surely meant leaving them all for dead, if they were even still alive at all at that point. It was something that had haunted him for five long years, and he'd been desperate for the chance to redeem himself.

Now here he was, taking that chance. Despite the possible dangers that his current patron had just presented to him, he knew without any further hesitation what his answer was.

"No, it wouldn't have made any difference at all," Jonas said. "I am completely in on this, no matter what or who we may encounter."

Efigenia smiled at that. Most of the rest of their drive was in silence.

CHAPTER THREE

After driving for just under an hour over increasingly less-maintained roads, they finally pulled over at the side and got out to prepare for the major part of their journey. Jonas recognized this particular area as not being that far from the initial staging area he'd used with Carter's expedition five years earlier, so they seemed to be off to a good start. In the past he had acted as a guide in the wilderness for many places all over the world, including Africa, the Middle East, and the Australian Outback, even Siberia on one very memorable but miserable occasion, but the Amazon Rainforest had been the most common one. However, the Amazon region was massive, and no matter how many times he had been here there was no way of saying that he was completely familiar with it all. Most of his journeys here had required him to stick to the western regions, which may have still been wild in areas but were at least closer to notable towns and cities. The expedition with Carter and her people had only been Jonas's second time hiking deep into the rainforest's eastern region, which was still far less explored.

Still, as they started out along their trek, Jonas felt like he should have had a better familiarity with this place. This was pretty close to where he had started when travelling with Carter, yet the area still felt strangely foreign to him. Maybe it was the trauma of everything that had happened the last time he was here that made it seem so alien. Maybe his brain had tried to erase any detailed memories of the terrain as a sort of safeguard against what had happened.

Efigenia must have seen him looking around quizzically at the environment, because she asked, "Is there anything familiar about any of this so far?"

"I don't know," Jonas said. "A lot has changed since I was last here. I remember landmarks, specific trees or rock formations, but there's no guarantee that they're still going to be here."

"You didn't keep any detailed maps?"

"We did, as in the expedition did, but I wasn't the one holding the majority of them. That was… that was Carter."

They walked for a while in silence, with Jonas

brooding on his many past mistakes, before Efigenia spoke again. "Did you know Arlene Carter or the rest of her team well, or was that the first time you'd worked with them?"

"I didn't know any of them well at all, but I was familiar with most of them. I respected them. I was… well, I guess I was attracted to Carter, but I never dreamed of trying to act on it. It wouldn't have been professional."

"Do you know if she felt the same way back?" Efigenia asked.

"Doesn't matter if she did or didn't," Jonas said. "As I said, wouldn't have been professional. She hired me to do a job, and that's where the relationship had to begin and end."

"Is that a strict rule you would follow with all your clients?" she asked. Jonas thought he could detect a bit of a flirty suggestion in her words.

"For as long as they were my clients, yes," he said. "Once the job was over, well, that could be different." He thought about what he had just said, and then added, "That was not intended as a suggestion, by the way."

Efigenia flashed him a wry smile. "Oh, of course not."

It wasn't long before they lost anything that

could easily be called a path, and it was time for Jonas to break out the machete and hack their way through some of the brush. Despite the landscape not feeling familiar to him, he quickly found himself feeling once more back in his element. For quite some time there wasn't a lot to worry about, and when night came they made camp and built a small fire. As they settled in to eat, Jonas figured this was a good time to get more information.

"So tell me more about this so-called lost city. I've heard legends about a Lost City of Z before, but I don't know a lot about the specific stories."

"Well, Fawcett was responsible for most of the stories, or at least the people following in Fawcett's footsteps and beliefs were. There were still a few people who continued to insist the city had to be out there even after Kuhikugu was found, but the more time passed the more those people were considered to be crackpots and lunatics. Before them, the only known reference was Manuscript 512, and that has never been considered particularly reliable. It described a massive city with Graeco-Roman aspects to the architecture, something that obviously shouldn't exist anywhere in the Amazon Rainforest. It certainly wouldn't match the architecture of any known civilization that would have lived in this area. So my hypothesis is that, if it really is real, then it's far older than any civilization previously known to be here. It could be well over a thousand years old, maybe even two thousand. It would be far older than the Incan or Aztec empires, and may even be older than the Mayans. It would completely rewrite everything we think we know about ancient civilizations in South America, or maybe even in the entire world."

"What makes you think the accounts weren't just embellished?" Jonas asked. "That was a common enough thing in accounts from that time, especially since no one apparently even knows who wrote the manuscript. It could have just been written by some random crackpot or con man."

"Well, that's certainly a danger, and it's what most archeologists thought was the case with the differences between the account in Manuscript 512 and what they saw at Kuhikugu. They think someone did see it once, and either got creative in the details or passed it along by word of mouth until the whole story was wildly out of proportion to the truth. But the accounts in the second manuscript I found are from a different person than the first, and they seem to corroborate everything that 512 said. Also, there's the 'geological oddity' that you found while you were searching for Carter. Do you remember anything about what you saw that would imply possible ancient European influence? Or at the very least influence from a culture not previously recorded here?"

"Honestly no, but in all fairness I wasn't exactly looking for architecture at the time. I was looking for my paying clients who had apparently snuck off without telling me where they were going. My mind was not on any historical aspects of what I may or may not find."

"I suppose you probably don't know a lot of architecture types anyway," she said.

"Why would you say that?" Jonas asked.

"I mean, it's not exactly something you have much need to learn when you're hacking your way through a forest, right?"

"And you think that's all I can do? Take a machete to a bunch of vines, live off the land in far off places?"

"Well, I guess I kind of assumed."

"I have an education, you know. I'm not just a meathead alcoholic with a machete."

"I insulted you, didn't I? I'm sorry. I didn't mean that."

"It's fine," Jonas grumbled. "It's just that after I lost Carter's team, my name was mud in expedition circles, but all the schooling I'd done way back when I was younger didn't seem to help me get any new opportunities, either. I'd thought all the book knowledge I had would work as a back up to give me some different direction to go with my life, but all those doors seemed to be just as closed to me."

"So what kind of education do you have?" Efigenia asked.

"A masters in philosophy," Jonas said.

"How do you go from studying philosophy in college to making your living guiding people through the most hostile environments on the planet? The two paths don't seem to be especially well-connected."

"I studied philosophy because I liked it. Meanwhile, I became a survival guide because my father had been teaching me that kind of thing since I was a kid. We grew up in the woods in Alaska. I didn't have a lot of scholarships, so I saved up for school by plying my trade in the wilderness, mostly to clueless tourists from the lower forty-eight. It just so happened that by the time I was done with school, I had made enough of a name for myself that that just seemed like a better way to use my time, you know?"

"So you're a swashbuckling, world-traveling adventurer that also happens to have a masters of philosophy," Efigenia said with amusement. "I've got to say, that's not really what I or anyone else would have expected of you."

"I wouldn't call myself 'swashbuckling.' I've never even seen a swash, let alone buckled one."

"Funny, too," she said. She looked for a moment like she wanted to say more, and Jonas was convinced she was about to test his ethics and make a pass at him. If she did, he was going to have to politely turn her down. He liked her enough that he might take her up on a more romantic tryst under other circumstances, but his ethics and reputation were more important to him at this moment. Absolutely no fraternization now.

Thankfully she seemed to rethink this, and said to him over the campfire, "I think it's about time for us to sleep. Do you think we should do it in shifts?"

"Just to be on the safe side, yeah," Jonas said. "The wild animals that could get into the camp while we sleep could cause us a whole world of hurt. Why don't you take the first two hours of sleeping while I watch. We can switch out every two hours until sunrise."

"Sounds like a plan to me," she said, and she huddled up in her sleeping bag and fell asleep quickly.

During Jonas's watch there was very little to concern him, although at one point he did think he heard the roar of a big cat of some kind off in the far distance. Efigenia hadn't included any guns in their supplies, so if something were to try coming for them they would have to rely on the fire and his machete. However, he didn't think that would be much of a problem. At the two hour mark he woke Efigenia, who took over and adamantly watched over them for her allotted time. They continued to switch off, with the only problem being Jonas's nagging thirst for something that would get him blinding drunk. That urge might have been a problem in civilization, but here there was nothing available that could tempt him during his shifts. This plan went smoothly for most of the night.

The key word, however, was "most." Because when he awoke for the final time right at the crack of dawn, roused by the sound of what seemed like multiple footsteps, he found ten or so spears pointed directly at his head.

CHAPTER FOUR

While he was awake and aware immediately, it took Jonas a few moments for him to process what he was seeing. His immediate field of vision was just the spear points with no context to the image. He immediately ruled out the possibility that the owners of the spears had any connection to Graft-Horton. They would be using guns, after all. The spear points looked similar in make to some that he had seen local tribes in the area use in the past, so that seemed like the most likely option. However, there had been no sign of anyone else in the area when they had stopped to make camp. It seemed highly unlikely that they had just sat down for a rest in some native group's territory without any sign of it whatsoever.

Unless Jonas had missed some key details because he was addled from missing his alcohol, but he didn't think he was that far gone. Or at least he hoped he wasn't.

Someone said a couple of words to him, but they were in a language he didn't know. Slowly, making sure to not make any sudden movements and give anyone a reason to put a spear point in his throat, Jonas sat up from his bedroll.

Ten tribespeople with spears were immediately around him, and as he looked around he saw that there were an additional four around Efigenia, who was sitting on a nearby log. They were brandishing the spears at her as well, but while she seemed uneasy, she didn't look like she crossed the line into scared. Jonas took that as a good sign that maybe this wasn't as bad as it seemed. He saw her looking at something behind him, so Jonas carefully and cautiously turned to look.

At the edge of the clearing where they had camped, there was a large additional group of tribespeople packed together tightly. It was difficult to get an accurate idea of their total number, but Jonas's best estimate was that there had to be a total of forty or so people in this tribe, assuming the entire tribe was here. Since there was no additional sign of a village around them, the sight of this many, quite a few of whom seemed to be women and children that were not taking the attitude of warriors or protectors, struck him as extremely unusual.

"Are you okay?" Jonas asked Efigenia. The tribespeople surrounding him tensed as he spoke, but no one made any move on him.

"I'm fine," she said. "They arrived just a few minutes ago. One of them snuck up on me and forced me to be quiet while the others surrounded us, but they don't seem to actually be aggressive."

"It seems pretty unusual to me for all of these people to be out in the middle of the forest like this at this time of the morning, don't you think?" Jonas asked.

Efigenia nodded. "This isn't a hunting or scouting party. Most of these people look pretty scared, and some of them have wounds like there was recently a fight. I don't think they're actually from around here."

"Are they a tribe that you recognize?"

"No, and I did my best to research who lives in the area before we came out. So they must be some kind of uncontacted tribe that hasn't been identified yet."

"Are you able to speak their language?" Jonas asked.

"I can try, but if they're truly uncontacted, it could be different enough from other local dialects that I won't be able to."

Efigenia tried several languages that Jonas didn't recognize, one of which some of the tribespeople seemed to at least partially understand. The fact that she was able to somewhat communicate with them seemed to calm them down slightly, just enough that a few of them lowered their spears, but most stayed alert. She did her best to relay what little she was able to say back to Jonas. It was strange, he thought, that he hadn't met them on his first expedition through here, and he asked Efigenia about that. She passed on the question in a very halting fashion, peppered with lots of hand gestures to try to get her point across, and although it took some time it seemed that Efigenia was able to get a basic understanding of what they were trying to say.

"I think they're saying they only recently came into this area," she said. "They were driven out from where they were before. They say people came, but I'm having trouble understanding what they said the people did."

Jonas took stock of the various tribespeople surrounding them. A few of them still looked aggressive toward the two of them, but most of the tribe just seemed scared and confused. Only the ones immediately around them had weapons, while the others were carrying makeshift bags and sacks full of items that they'd been able to carry with them when they were forced out of where they had been before.

Something occurred to Jonas. "Can you ask them if the people who drove them out had tools or equipment with the logo of Graft-Horton?"

"Oh. Yes," Efigenia said. She reached into her pack to pull out a piece of paper and a pen. Quickly she scrawled out an approximation of the company's corporate logo, then showed it to the tribespeople. The reaction among them was immediate and agitated.

"I'm going to assume that means yes," Jonas said.

One of the elder members of the tribe, a man who had now brought his spear up to an unthreatening, upright position, started speaking quite animatedly, and even with Efigenia translating Jonas was able to realize that he seemed to be talking about bulldozers and various earthmovers, along with men carrying guns.

"So, what I'm putting together is that a large number of men just showed up one day and started destroying the village. They didn't have any warning that it was going to happen. Several of the tribespeople tried to fight back and got shot, or they were… I think they might be trying to say that some were arrested? If so, that would imply that Graft-Horton had some kind of police on their side, even though such an intrusion would not have been legal in the slightest."

Jonas looked at a few of the tribespeople who were still taking a more threatening stance toward them. "Are you able to tell them that we aren't in any way associated with Graft-Horton?"

"I'm getting the impression that they know that, but I don't know if that makes things any better. The bits and pieces of chatter that I'm picking up suggest that one or two of the people want to make examples of us."

"Then maybe it's best if you try to communicate that we're fully prepared to immediately pack up and be on our way with no further conflict between us."

Efigenia said something haltingly in the best she could approximate of their language. While several of the tribespeople seemed satisfied with what she said, others angrily said something back to her.

"I think we have permission to leave," Efigenia

said, "but I think there's enough dissent among them that we need to make it as quick as possible, just to be sure that we don't step on any toes."

"Then I suggest we get packing and move out as quickly as possible," Jonas said. "If nothing else, these people have already been through enough without having to worry about us hanging around, anyway."

They packed up their camp quickly, all the while being watched warily by the tribespeople. Efigenia did her best to exchange a few words with them and reassure them, but given everything that had happened to them it wasn't surprising that they seemed unreceptive of her attempts at small talk in a language she only sort-of seemed to understand. They seemed quite relieved when the two of them were ready to go, and Jonas was just as happy to leave them be.
"Do you know if they're planning on staying here," Jonas asked, "or do they intend to keep moving?"

Efigenia said a few words, and the elder who'd spoken earlier made gestures that they intended to keep moving deeper into the forest.

"As best as I can tell, they seem to think that finding us here is a sign that they aren't safe yet,"

Efigenia said. “They look like they’ll keep moving, but they won’t be heading the same direction as us.”

“That’s good,” Jonas said. “Just in case Graft-Horton really is sending an expedition this way, the two groups hopefully shouldn’t run into each other.”

“Maybe I can warn them that others may be coming,” she said, then spoke a few words. The tone the elder used in response sounded gracious and thankful, and then he gestured for them to leave.

Jonas and Efigenia started moving, each of them occasionally looking back to see what the tribespeople were doing. They may have been starting to take a rest, but there continued to be a worried air about them that suggested they wouldn’t stay there for long.

“Is that something that’s been happening more and more?” Jonas asked. “The locals being forced out of their land by Graft-Horton?”

“It happens a lot more than anyone wants to admit, even without Graft-Horton in the mix,” Efigenia said. “There’s been more reports of it recently though, although most of those reports get buried by the local media or authorities. For every atrocity they perform against a tribe that we hear about, though, there are probably ten that they've successfully covered up. I've had colleagues that have tried to help, but most of them seem to stop mysteriously in the middle of their efforts, like they've either been threatened and are frightened into silence, or they've been paid off."

"Has anyone from Graft-Horton tried to get to you?" Jonas asked. "Maybe tried to bribe you into silence regarding the possible existence of Z?"

"No, and that actually strikes me as something worrisome," she said. "I have a reputation of putting my work first above all else, but even with that you would think Graft-Horton would have tried something. Even threatening anonymous notes or phone calls, but there's been nothing like that. Except for my anonymous contact in the organization, they practically act like I don't exist."

"Hmm. That does support the hypothesis that your contact is actually some kind of trick or trap. Have you taken any precautions just in case it is?"

"I have people that know where I'm going this week, and I have tell-all papers ready to be sent out to key people if I just so happen to go missing or disappear. But beyond that, what could I even do?"

"You could have brought a gun. I didn't see one anywhere in any of the equipment you packed."

"Just because you didn't see it doesn't mean I don't have one." She stopped walking and pulled up her shirt. There was a small revolver strapped to her side. He had to admit that she wore it well. He hadn't even suspected it was there up until this very moment.

"It's not much, but it's better than nothing," Jonas said. "I couldn't exactly bring one with me on the plane. I don't suppose you thought to bring a second for me, just in case, did you?"

She shook her head. "I only own the one, and I couldn't get another on such short notice. It's loaded and I have six more bullets in my pocket, but that's all I've got, so we'd better hope we don't need to use it for anything."

Jonas sure hoped not, but he doubted that was going to be the case. Given what little he had seen so far regarding what Graft-Horton could and would do to those who stood in their way, he suspected that sooner or later that gun would need to be used.

CHAPTER FIVE

They made their way through the rainforest for well over an hour after that with nothing particularly noteworthy occurring. The two of them chatted a little bit, mostly about inconsequential things, but mostly they stayed silent, saving their breath instead for the effort it took to hack their way through the foliage and hike over uneven terrain. The forest around them teemed with life, and Jonas was glad to once again be surrounded by the sounds of the wilderness. He'd forgotten how much he missed the simply sensory inputs that came with trekking through lands far from civilization.

Although gladness wasn't the only thing he felt as they continued along. There was another feeling he'd had since the flight, and it had been slowly growing ever since. He'd been able to ignore it for a while in the night, and his adrenaline at waking up with spears pointed at him had kept him going and helped him forget for a while after they woke up. However, it was coming on him strong again. He thought he was hiding the misery it caused him well enough, but after a while Efigenia finally spoke up and let him know that she'd been seeing it all along.

"It's withdrawal, isn't it?" she asked. "From the booze you've been using to keep yourself going for these last five years."

"You know, when I was getting ready to come down here, I kept trying to tell myself that this wouldn't be a problem," Jonas said. "That I hadn't become so reliant on it that I would have a problem going without it. I guess we never really talked when you first contacted me about whether or not you knew this would be a concern."

"If you want me to be honest, I was very aware of the drinking problem you've developed. When I asked around about you, every single person I talked to warned me that your alcohol use had gotten serious and that I should try to find someone else to help me."

"Why didn't you, then?" Jonas asked. "If that's what everyone was saying, then why not try someone else? Is it just because I had the knowledge others might not?"

"Again, being honest, that was most of it. You may in fact be the only living person on Earth who has actually seen the Lost City of Z."

"Only most of it?" Jonas thought of that for a second. He wasn't offended by what she said. In fact, he was refreshed that she hadn't tried to hide that she might have had reservations about him. "You know, if you had hired me just for that knowledge and then a second person to actually act as a proper guide for the jungle, I would have understood. It might have hurt, but I would have understood."

"And I probably could have fit that into the budget. In fact I had planned to do just that all the way up until our Zoom call together. That was when I decided I wouldn't need anyone else."

"And what exactly brought you to that conclusion?"

"All the research I did on what you were like before the incident with Carter's expedition suggested you were among the best in the business. And on that call, I looked into your eyes and I could still see that person there. I could tell you wanted it, the chance to redeem yourself. I still see it right now, even though you're obviously struggling. And that's why I still believe you're the best person to help me. I don't think that person you used to be ever really went away. You just think he did."

Jonas couldn't think of anything to say to that. He certainly didn't feel like that person he used to be, and yet…

He stopped in mid-thought and came to an abrupt halt. Efigenia was close enough behind him that she almost ran into him.

"Jonas?" she asked. "Is something…"

"Shhh," he said. "I just… give me a second."

Growing up on the edge of the wilderness in Alaska, one of the things he had learned to do without actually realizing he was doing it was to keep a constant awareness of everything in his environment. In any jungle or forest, there were thousands of things in someone's immediate vicinity that could be either helpful or harmful in any situation, and it was an important skill to develop the sort of instincts that could recognize those things before even the conscious mind was aware of them. He was feeling those instincts go off now. In his better days he might have been able to identify what set them off faster, but the withdrawal was playing just enough havoc with him that he was sluggish in picking up the signs.

The area immediately surrounding them had a gap in the trees, a small clearing that gave him a mostly unobstructed view all around them for a radius of between five and ten feet in any direction. The clearing was swampy, probably at the edge of a river or a flood plain just beyond their current line of sight. There was a fallen log off to one side, and several thick areas of bushes around them, all of which could have been hiding something. He listened closely to the sounds of the rainforest: birds in the distance, maybe some kind of tree-dwelling mammal nearby, but nothing that seemed that close. In his experience, those kinds of things only made themselves scarce when they felt there was one or more threats nearby. It was possible that the animals registered the two humans traipsing through the brush to be that threat, but Jonas still felt like there had to be something else. He paid careful attention to his instincts, and they drew his eyes back to the log. It was just hidden enough in the brush that he couldn't see any part of it too clearly other than some mottled colors, but it occurred to him that, with no tree or stump directly around it, there was no actual good reason for it to be there.

Finally, after several very tense seconds of waiting, Jonas's suspicions were confirmed and the "log" moved. As it moved, the mottled coloring that had initially disguised it as some kind of fallen tree could now be seen as more dynamic and patterned. It also looked far thicker than what he had initially suspected.

"What is it?" Efigenia asked.

"Anaconda, I think," Jonas said quietly. "No sudden movements."

The enormous snake was a greenish-brown in color, and while it bore some resemblance to other anacondas Jonas had seen both in captivity and the wild, he suspected it may have been of some previously undocumented variety. The biggest anaconda he had previously seen would have been able to take down a very large dog, but this one was big enough that he could easily see it making a snack out of a human if it worked for its meal.

"What are we going to do?" Efigenia asked.

"We just stay put until it goes along its way. We're hopefully big enough that it won't see us as prey, and maybe as long as we keep still it will think we're trees or something."

He heard something rustling in the undergrowth nearby, and at first he thought that was also from the snake. But the more he paid attention, the more he realized the sound was coming from a completely different direction. And it was a sound similar to something he had heard before on one particularly tense trip into the Amazon Rainforest.

The anaconda wasn't the only predator in the vicinity that had spooked the wildlife.

"Efigenia, I think we need to get out of here," Jonas said.

"What happened to 'no sudden movements?'" she asked.

"I think there's about to be a whole lot of sudden movements whether we like it or not," he said. "When I say so, start running back along the path we just cut, and maybe we can…" But as he heard the brush shifting again, he realized that wouldn't be a safe direction to go. The thing he had heard was now behind them, meaning that the only way away from it was through the rough, uncleared area in the clearing… and right in the direction of the anaconda. Jonas remembered what Efigenia had said on the Zoom call about Percy Fawcett's claim of having shot a sixty-foot anaconda during his journeys, and while that remained a wild and unbelievable claim, this one here was probably the largest Jonas had ever seen in his travels, at roughly thirty-five or more feet.

And if he was right about what was causing the

noises behind them, then the anaconda might possibly have been the lesser of the two dangers surrounding them.

Efigenia, while maybe not as proficient as he was in working through the dangers of the untraveled portions of the Amazon, must have known enough from her field work that she began to recognize what else might currently be stalking them.

"That's a jaguar, isn't it?" she asked quietly.

"Listen, I think we can get out of this, but we'll have to do something that might sound a little crazy," Jonas said. "When I say go, I want you to run as fast as the brush will allow you in that direction." He indicated a slightly less overgrown spot that still took them uncomfortably close to the anaconda. "And it probably wouldn't be a great idea to look back."

"Won't that startle the snake?" Efigenia asked.

"I need you to trust me on this," Jonas said. "I know that my reputation from the last five years might lead you to not do so, and my current condition might inspire even less confidence, but I'm hoping that my reputation from before that is enough to convince you that I know what I'm doing."

"Okay. I trust you."

"Annnnd… go!"

Between the heaviness of their gear and the terrain, their fastest speed wasn't going to be that fast at all, but Jonas was hoping that wouldn't matter. Instead he was relying on the sudden flurry of movement to both attract and distract the two predators they were caught between. Behind them, he could hear a sudden burst of movement through the underbrush as the jaguar sprang at them. In his mind time slowed down, and the pounce of the enormous cat felt inevitable, an inescapable fate. Then there was another noise, the quick rustling of underbrush as another predator saw the flurry of movement and chose that moment to strike.

There was a loud hiss and a horrific screech from the jaguar. While Jonas knew it wasn't the best idea, he couldn't help but look back over his shoulder, and while he knew he should keep running, he still found himself slowing down to take in the unbelievable spectacle taking place back the way they had come.

The anaconda had attacked the jaguar, just like he'd hoped. Its mouth was clamped on the jaguar's neck, and it quickly moved its enormous bulk to wrap around the jungle cat. The jaguar itself was of an impressive size, perhaps not the biggest Jonas had ever seen but definitely close. That made the size of the anaconda all the more horrifying, as its actual dimensions became more apparent as its coils squeezed the jaguar. Jonas's initial assessment that it was about thirty-five feet long, which alone would have made it the largest anaconda ever put on record, now seemed to be on the small side. The mucky water in the clearing had apparently hidden most of the anaconda's bulk, and he now had to estimate that it was more like forty to fifty feet. Suddenly Percy Fawcett's ridiculous assertions about the snake he had shot seemed a little more realistic.

As much as Jonas had a morbid curiosity and wanted to watch the rest of what happened next, his survival instincts got the better of him. In truth the two of them were probably safe now; the anaconda would have to take quite some time to squeeze the jaguar into cardiac arrest, and then it would be hours for it to swallow something that size. Afterward the snake would be lethargic from its big meal, and probably wouldn't even need to eat again for a couple of weeks. But there was still the slight danger in sticking around. If the anaconda perceived them as a threat, it could still let the broken jaguar loose and come after them. It was better to get as far away from here as possible.

He motioned to Efigenia to continue running, and the two of them left this gruesome tableau behind them.

CHAPTER SIX

They kept moving at an accelerated pace for longer than they probably needed before they finally stopped to catch their breath. There was a near zero chance that the anaconda wanted to or was capable of pursuing them, but just to be certain Jonas checked to make sure that nothing had followed them. Once he was positive of this, he declared that they were stopping for a food and bathroom break. Efigenia was too tired to say anything against it, although he knew she would rather keep going if that was possible. At the very least, they needed to regain themselves a little after the terror and adrenaline rush of what they had just witnessed.

"Never in any of my time studying in the field have I ever seen anything like that," Efigenia said.

"Got to say that I haven't either. How the hell does an anaconda get to be that big?"

"It's too bad we weren't able to get any pictures or footage," she said. "I bet National Geographic would have loved to buy something like that."

"They can't buy anything from someone that's been eaten," Jonas said. "We were damned lucky. I can't begin to count the number of ways that could have ended with both of us dead."

"Yeah," she started to say. "Uh, I suppose, yeah…" She interrupted herself by doubling over and vomiting into a bush. Jonas rushed over and held her hair out of the way so none of it got caught in the stream. After several heaves she was able to make herself stop, but it was another few minutes before she was able to stand up straight again.

"I'm sorry for that," she finally managed to say. "It's just… that's the first time out in the rainforest that I ever thought I might actually die. Is that… is that something you've experienced before?"

"Not exactly in that way, but yeah," he said.

"And those times, they don't cause you nightmares or anything?"

"I never said that. Even before what happened with Carter and her team, I used to have nightmares all the time."

"If I had things like that happen to me on a regular basis," Efigenia said, "I would probably drink too. Er, sorry, that was probably insensitive of me."

"Maybe it was, but it's also true. Truth be told, I was probably always just one big traumatic experience away from burying myself in the bottle. The Carter Incident just happened to be the one that finally did it."

"I bet you never threw up afterward, though," she said.

"Eh, don't be too sure. You might be surprised. Here, have some water to wash the taste out of your mouth."

They didn't do a lot of talking as they took their rest, as brief as it ended up being. While Jonas thought it might do Efigenia good to stop for longer, she insisted, once they had eaten and relieved themselves, that they had to keep going. She was a tough one, Jonas realized, something that a lot of people around her in academia probably never would have recognized. He found it admirable.

They weren't going again for very long when Efigenia again motioned for them to stop. Jonas thought at first that she had rethought the idea of taking a longer break, but then he saw that her attention had been drawn to something deep within the trees. "Is this the same path you were on when you were with Carter?" she asked.

"No, I would guess that we were about a mile or two west of here. Why?"

"At any point on your journey to where you eventually lost them, did she ask you to stop so that she could investigate anything?"

"No. Again, why?"

"Because it's possible we might have just found something she never got a chance to see." She started to walk off in the direction she'd been looking without even waiting for Jonas and his machete to clear a path. However terrified she might have been earlier with the anaconda and the jaguar, all fear seemed to have left her now as her entire mind was taken up with curiosity over whatever it was she thought she'd seen.

Jonas rushed ahead of her so that he could work on clearing the path, and soon they found themselves at a large outcropping of rock in an area where no other such rock formations seemed to be. He thought about what she had said about the rock face he'd seen five years ago and how there was no way it could have been natural, but just like then, this rock formation was so overgrown with plants that he wouldn't have thought twice about it under most circumstances. It was about ten feet high and mostly flat, leaning forward at an angle with several vines hanging over it. The only way that Efigenia could have possibly noticed this was if she had intentionally been looking for things just like this.

"What do you think it is?" Jonas asked.

"If there really was a city out here somewhere, no matter how long ago, there had to be roads or paths to get to it. Those roads would be long gone, but I was hoping for some kind of signage or way marker that would have been found along it. This could be one of those." She held her hand out to him. "Give me the machete. Let's see if all this vegetation might be hiding something."

The plant matter was incredibly thick, but after five or more minutes of consistent hacking they were able to see the actual face of the stone, and sure enough, there was something hidden here. The stone was worn in some places, but the vegetation seemed to have actually protected a lot of the fine chiseling and sculpting that had been done to it. At just under twenty feet wide, it depicted a number of stylized figures and symbols. At first glance the only thing that Jonas immediately recognized were carvings of what looked like fish. Efigenia got so close that her nose was almost touching the stone as she investigated further.

“This art here doesn’t make sense,” Efigenia said. “We’re a long way from most parts of the Amazon River, but these fish look like piranhas. I suppose it wouldn’t be too much to assume that people in this region still knew what they were, but at the same time I don’t know any reason why anyone would feel the need to depict them in this area.”

Jonas moved closer to the stonework. He could definitely see the piranhas in this, but that wasn’t the only thing the relief depicted. There were some crudely rendered creatures that might have been bugs or spiders, maybe even scorpions of some sort, and something that might have been a mountain in the background. Underneath the shadow of the mountain there was a crude depiction of great walls, and within them a number of structures, some like pyramids, others unlike anything that was traditionally believed to have ever existed in this area.

“I think these may be some kind of instructions on how to get to Z,” Jonas said. “Like a map.”

“No, I don’t think… wait. Maybe you’re right,”

Efigenia said. She took off her backpack and pulled out a few photos of satellite images of the region. "Some of the markings on this stonework might correspond to a few regions on the map, but there's a lot that doesn't."

"A couple of things you need to remember," Jonas said as he traced his finger along a line that he hoped was supposed to be some kind of path. "The first is that they didn't have access to your fancy maps there. Whichever civilization built Z, they could have had cartographers, but even if they did there's no way of telling how accurate their measurements might have been. The second is that was somewhere between five hundred and a thousand years ago, right? Terrain changes. There are landslides, rivers flood and change course. Lots of stuff will be different."

"But it can't be this different," she said. She pointed at a couple of areas in the satellite images. "See all these rolling hills and small mountains in this part? This stone work makes it look like they don't even exist. A lot of time may have passed, but not enough for that sort of geological transformation."

While she puzzled over the inconsistencies, Jonas found his eye being drawn to something on the far side of the stone wall. A lot of it was still covered with vines that he had to hack away with his machete, but after he did he found a strange pattern similar to a checkerboard. A small number of squares on the checkerboard were marked with an X.

"We should get some pictures of all this," Jonas said. "We might need to reference them later."

"Yeah, great idea," Efigenia said. "We'll need to make sure this area is well marked on our maps, too, so I can send someone out in the future to further study this stonework." She took out her camera and started taking pictures while Jonas, on a hunch, found some thin paper and used a pencil to make a rubbing of the checkerboard design. It took several pages for him to get the entire thing copied, but he wanted to be able to look at it more closely later and with more detail than he might be able to get from a photograph.

Efigenia pulled out a compass and, after looking several times between it, the rough map in the stone, and some satellite images she had with her, she finally said, "If this art is to be believed, then we've been going in the generally correct direction, but we need to adjust slightly to the north."

Jonas had to take a moment to consider this. "If that's the direction you wish to go, then we can go that way."

"Do I sense disapproval in your voice?"

"It's not the direction I went with Carter," Jonas said. "My impression was that you were interested in recreating my journey with her in order to re-find that wall I may or may not have come across. What's the point in having me here if we go in a completely different direction?"

She looked for a moment like she was going to say something irritated back to him, but after a few seconds of hesitation her expression changed to one of thoughtfulness.

"Listen, I understand that the reason you're here doing this is different than the reason I'm here," she said. "You've got something to prove. But the evidence directly in front of us is leading us somewhere slightly different, and that's the lead I want to follow."

Jonas took a deep breath and nodded. "You're the one who'll be handing the paycheck out when this is over. We'll go the direction you want."

By this time the sun was getting low in the sky, and in other normal circumstances it would have been his standard practice to start searching for a good spot to camp for the night. However, given Efigenia's sense of urgency, they soldiered on for a while longer. They didn't pause again until Jonas heard her cursing behind him.

"Shit! Shit, shit, shit!" She then added a few more curse words in her own language, as well as what seemed to be two or three others.

He stopped and looked back at her. "What is it?"

"My gun," she said, lifting her shirt just enough for both of them to see that it was missing from where she'd been hiding it. "It's gone."

"Any idea how far back you might have lost it?" Jonas asked.

"Last time I was sure I had it was back before the anaconda," she said. "I suppose it's possible I lost it since then, but…"

"But there's no way to tell where," Jonas finished for her, "and the amount of ground we've covered since then is too great. As much as we might wish we had it later, we can't go back looking for it now."

"Crap," she said, then checked her pockets. "I still have the extra bullets, but that's not going to do us a lot of good without a gun to fire them with."

That was when they heard the voices somewhere in the distance behind them, and the language was definitely not the displaced tribespeople from earlier.

It appeared they were no longer alone on their path.

CHAPTER SEVEN

Jonas exchanged a look with Efigenia, and it was clear from her expression that she was thinking the same thing he was: if this wasn't the tribe they had met, then the only group of people who would have any business being out this far in the wilderness, and right on their tail for that matter, would be people from Graft-Horton. If they weren't being terribly quiet about coming through the forest, then they probably didn't realize that the two of them were ahead of them, or at least not that they were so close.

That meant that they had a decision to make with almost no time to make it. They could either try to hide and wait for the group to go past, which would be safer but would let the Graft-Horton folks have a lead on the trail of Z, or they could get moving as fast as they could and try to stay ahead of them. In that case, however, they would be more likely to give away that they were even in the vicinity, which could prove deadly if they were really as murderous as Efigenia thought they were.

Neither was a great option, but it was possible they had an advantage. If the Graft-Horton people hadn't found the same marker that they had, then they might not have the same clues as to where to go. With that knowledge, as well as Jonas's expertise in the wilderness, it was possible they might be able to get some distance between them.

He motioned for Efigenia to keep going, but also held up his finger to his lips in a shushing gesture. He had no idea what quality of trackers or guides Graft-Horton might have with them, but if they were lucky, Jonas would be better.

They got moving, keeping a brisk pace, and soon the sounds of the people following them started to fade. As they went along, though, Jonas found the potential paths ahead of them narrowing. The earth around them was slowly rising up on either side so that they seemed to be at the bottom of some kind of ravine, or maybe it was some kind of path or road that had at one point been cut into the land. The path between the rocks was wide enough that a horse or mule-drawn wagon could have gone down it, and the rock walls on either side were high enough that someone could have used them to keep watch of anyone coming or going. Or possibly could have set up an ambush for them.

"I didn't see any of this when I was here five years ago," Jonas said. He spoke just loud enough for Efigenia to hear him, but tried to keep it low enough that it wouldn't carry to anyone that might be behind them.

"We're definitely on the path directed by the marker we found," Efigenia quietly said back. "None of this can possibly be natural. Someone created this path."

"Yeah, and made sure it was defensible."

"If we had time," she said, "this would be somewhere I would want to stop and study. All of this has to be…"

There was a loud, pained creak of wood beneath their feet. Before, they had been walking on stone or dirt covered in vegetation, but now, beneath both of them, the sounds of their footsteps echoed as if they were suddenly on a wooden bridge, and not one that was particularly stable.

"Efigenia, stop," Jonas said. "Don't move."

They'd been so caught up in the idea of getting away from who was behind them, and so enraptured by the peculiar road and structure around it, that they hadn't been paying enough attention to where they'd been stepping. Now, Jonas shifted his weight ever so slightly from one foot to the other and listened to how much the wood beneath them moaned at the weight. He looked down and gently nudged some of the vegetation with his toes to reveal and confirm the wooden planks beneath them. Now that he was paying attention, he could see that hidden beneath the overgrowth there was a square section of roughly ten feet by ten feet that the wood covered. The wood seemed extremely old and brittle, and judging by the springiness of it, didn't seem to have anything directly beneath it.

"What is it?" Efigenia asked.

"I think we just stepped on a trap."

"Can't, uh, can't we just step off it? Or would that trigger it?"

Theoretically they should have just been able to get off it, he thought, if only the wood had been new and sturdy. And indeed, if the wood they stood on had lasted all the way since Z had been inhabited, then at one point it must have been thick and sturdy indeed, more so than he would have thought possible for the time. But the wood was rotten, and they had just put both of their full body weights on it, putting stress on the wood that it likely had not experienced for hundreds of years. The fact that it hadn't already given out beneath them was practically a miracle, and even the slightest shift of weight could make that miracle suddenly become a curse for them.

Even with neither of them moving, the wood groaned at their weight. The wrong move might break the wood and send them falling through, but staying here too long was definitely going to result in the same fate.

"Okay, listen," Jonas said, trying to sound as calm as possible. "We can either both try jumping off at the same time, or we can try to reduce our weight first."

"With how much gear we're carrying, I don't know if jumping that distance would even be possible," Efigenia said. "What if we take our packs off and throw them to safety, then try doing it?"

"Alright then. We'll have to move slowly and deliberately," Jonas said. "And we should do it one at a time. I have the heavier gear in mine, so I'll go first." Efigenia nodded. All the muscles in her jaw were taut, and Jonas could see how absolutely terrified she was, but she was holding her emotions in well.

As Jonas carefully slipped off the straps of his pack, he looked down and tried to get a better idea of the construction of whatever they were standing on. The wooden platform looked like it might have consisted of two main sheets of wood, and there were worn nubs just poking out of the underbrush that might have been hinges of some kind, although they were of a different make and style than anything he would have seen in the modern world. It seemed to Jonas that they were probably standing on some kind of trapdoor that would swing inward and drop anyone standing on it, but whatever was supposed to trigger it to open hadn't gone off.

He had no idea what would be below the trapdoor, but there was no way it was something he actually wanted to see.

The wood creaked threateningly as he slowly removed the pack. There was a distinct possibility that doing this could in fact shift the weight in such a way to crack the trapdoor, but Jonas tried not to think about that as he swung the pack and let it go. It made an arc through the air and landed on the side of the trapdoor opposite of the direction they had come. It wouldn't do them any good for their gear to be on the wrong side if and when they were able to make it across.

"You next," Jonas said. "Carefully but slowly."

Efigenia nodded and started to undo the buckles holding her pack in place. The wood didn't make any sounds as she did this, and Jonas started to think this was something they'd be able to get through without any further problems.

From somewhere back down the path they had come, there was a gunshot.

Everything that came next happened very fast, but Jonas felt like he saw and heard it all despite the raging headache he was still feeling from his withdrawal. Something that sounded like a bullet ricocheted off the rock walls around them, signaling that, whoever it was that had just fired, was very clearly aiming at them. The sound startled Efigenia as she was slipping off her pack, and the pack dropped from her hands directly onto the rotten wood at their feet. The instant the heavy pack hit, the wood shattered, and both of them dropped into a pit underneath. Jonas's hands had already started reaching for the pack to try to catch it, but he wasn't fast enough. His hands were out in front of him, though, which was fortuitous as he started to drop. He tried to grab the lip of the pit they were falling into, but he missed, instead firmly wrapping them in some roots poking through the pit's wall a few feet below the pit's top ledge. Next to him, Efigenia also tried to reach out, and one of her hands got a hold on a rough spot in the pit wall while the other one gripped and tugged at his shirt. Both of them had grips, but they were tenuous at best.

Below them, Efigenia's pack and the broken pieces of the trapdoor splashed into a pool of water. It was about ten feet down from Jonas's feet, and the disturbance caused something below the dark surface to churn in a frenzy. Jonas suddenly had a very dark suspicion about what was swimming around down there at the bottom of the pit.

"Efigenia, whatever you do, don't let go," he said. "I think we've found why there were piranhas in that stonework."

"But how did they get here?" she asked. "We're at least thirty miles from the nearest…"

"Can we save any attempt at scientific analysis for later? Right now I'm kind of trying to concentrate."

The wall onto which they were both clinging was made of some kind of stone or brickwork, and while it had probably been of a very fine craftsmanship when this shaft was first constructed, hundreds of years of the elements meant that Jonas could feel it all ready to give out beneath their weight, and the roots by which he had an additional grip didn't feel terribly strong. He looked up for more handholds and footholds they could use to climb back up, and there were a few places where the bricks were missing that might work, but mostly it was too smooth. He personally had enough strength and stamina to climb back up, he thought, but he wasn't sure if he could say the same for Efigenia.

From up above them, something caused a silhouette against the sky, and Jonas looked all the way to the mouth of the shaft. While there was a lot of shadow on the man standing at the top, Jonas still felt like there was something recognizable about him, like maybe he had seen this person on some news show or on the internet.

While Jonas wasn't able to put a name to the man's face, Efigenia seemed to know who he was instantly. "Graft? Cristof Graft?"

The man didn't seem terribly surprised to be recognized. "Miss Araujo. I wasn't expecting you to be out here in the jungle in time."

"Graft, I have no idea what you're doing out

here yourself, but you have to help us up. I think those are piranhas down there!" Jonas wasn't sure if she really expected him to help or if she was just grasping at straws, but either way Graft didn't seem very amenable to the idea.

"Oh. Well then, I hope they're hungry, so it makes your deaths as quick and painless as possible."

"What the fuck?" she asked. "Graft, quit screwing around. Help! Is anyone else up there?"

Another man appeared next to Graft, a young and gangly person that didn't seem at all comfortable to be in the position he was next to the billionaire. He was even more uncomfortable as he looked down at the two people clinging to the side of the shaft, but he didn't look like he was going to do anything further to help.

"Whoever you are, please, you've got to help us," Efigenia said.

"I'm afraid Mr. Schulz here won't be helping you, even if you thought he was doing that earlier," Graft said.

"Huh?" she asked. "I don't understand."

"I… I'm sorry," the young man said to her, then backed away from the ledge and disappeared from their view.

"You see," Graft said, "Schultz was the source of your insider information within my organization. I instructed him to reach out to you knowing that if we followed you we would start off in the right direction, and when the right time came I could have you killed before you even knew we were behind you. Earlier, one of my subordinates seems to have given away that you were being followed, unfortunately. But it looks like we won't even have to dirty our hands with your blood. You seem to have done that all by yourself."

Graft stepped back away from the top of the hole. There were some awkward shuffling sounds as Graft and his people carefully moved around the edge of the pit, but those sounds quickly faded as the group left, leaving Jonas and Efigenia to wait for their strength to give out.

CHAPTER EIGHT

Jonas assessed the section of wall that he was dangling from. Maybe it was indeed possible that he could climb up, but Efigenia likely didn't have his same level of body strength. If he tried to go up, he could do so, but it would mean leaving her behind. Maybe, once he was at the top, he would find something that would help her up as well, but his brain rejected that idea completely out of hand. Leaving her behind in any capacity for any length of time felt to him like abandonment, and five years of guilt over the last time he had abandoned somebody was enough for a lifetime. Either he was going to get out of this shaft with her next to him, or he wasn't going to get out at all.

"How much longer do you think you can hold on?" Jonas asked her.

"My hands are cramping up," she said with a distinct quiver of fear in her voice. "I don't think I can do this for much longer."

"Do you think you would be able to hold on longer if you were on my back than if you were trying to cling to the wall?"

"Yeah, I think so, but there's no way you would be able to climb out with me weighing you down."

Jonas looked down at the rest of the pit below them. While the water itself was dark, he could see the piranhas churning near the surface. They seemed to be most distracted at the moment by the contents of Efigenia's pack, which had included a sizable portion of their food, but he didn't think he could count on that distraction to save them if they fell in.

There has to be a way, he thought. *Think. Maybe there's other handholds. Someone had to construct this shaft, right? And they had to be able to get in and out. Some semblance of that escape route must still be here even after all this time.*

While it was fairly dark near the bottom of the shaft where the waterline was, Jonas still thought he could see something in the shadows. It suddenly occurred to him that it was unlikely for the piranhas to be able to survive only at the bottom of one pit for hundreds or thousands of years. There had to be some kind of water system or sewer system that connected this pit to somewhere else, allowing the piranhas to move about and thrive and find food elsewhere. That dark spot he saw might just be some kind of service shaft or tunnel that led somewhere else. If he went for it and he was wrong about what it was, that would likely be their end. But if he was right…

"I've got a desperate idea," Jonas said. "Try to get on my back, but do it carefully. I need to keep a grip as well."

It was a harrowing process for her to transfer her hold from the wall to him, and although she wasn't the largest woman, holding her weight was quite taxing on him. There had been times in his adventures when he'd been forced to carry enough gear on his back that it would be comparable to her, but some of those muscles had atrophied in the previous five years. Finally she managed to have a good solid hold on him, with her arms clasped tightly around his chest and her legs wrapped awkwardly around his waist. He wasn't going to be able to hold this for long, but hopefully he didn't have to.

"Okay, I'm going to start climbing down now," he said. "Make sure you…"

"Down!? How the hell is getting closer to the piranhas going to get us out of here?"

"Please, I just need you to trust me. Make sure you hold on, but if I tell you to let go or do something that doesn't make sense, you need to do it without question. I'm running out of stamina and don't have time to be quizzed, got it?"

She took a deep breath. "Okay then. I trust you."

Jonas began the painstaking process of finding hand and footholds as he worked his way down closer to the piranha-infested water. Mostly this kind of climbing came back to him surprisingly easy, but from the glance he had gotten at the dark space below earlier, the hard part wouldn't be climbing down but rather changing the walls he was on. The wall he seemed to want was on the opposite side of the ten-foot rectangle they were in. If he were in better condition or didn't have someone clinging to his back, he might have tried to jump the gap, but even if he was willing to be that reckless with his own life, he wasn't going to put his client in danger again.

Several times as he went down and around he had a moment where the ancient stonework either crumbled when he went to grip it or else it just didn't provide any place for him to find purchase. In each instance he had to keep himself from panicking, and he kept having to concentrate just to keep himself from shaking from exertion. However, after an unknown time of meticulous and careful movement, Jonas finally found himself just above the water and next to that spot of shadow he'd seen earlier.

As he'd suspected, the dark area was the mouth of a tunnel. It had a round opening, with the lower lip just slightly under water, meaning that the bottom of the tunnel was wet but not quite deep enough at the moment for piranhas to swim in it. It wasn't very wide, perhaps just a little bit more than the width of his shoulders. It would be a tight fit for him, although less so for Efigenia.

"Okay, you see the tunnel?" he asked her. "I'm going to need you to carefully climb off my back and into it."

"There's water in it. The piranhas will still be able to get us."

"I don't think it's deep enough for them at the moment, and even if it is in a few places, there will only be one or two piranhas for us to deal with at a time rather than an entire pool of them."

"Where does the tunnel even go?" she asked.

"I don't know and right now I don't care. Efigenia, I need you to get off my back as soon as possible. I feel like my grip might be going."

Without any further word Efigenia moved one of her feet down to the lip of the tunnel. Just outside the lip a few piranhas could be seen moving near the surface, obviously waiting for the moment where she screwed up and fell in. There was a moment where it looked like she might be about to lose her balance, and Jonas had the horrible realization that if that occurred there was absolutely nothing he would be able to do to steady her. However, after nearly a minute of tense and careful movements, Efigenia was just inside the tunnel. She moved deeper quickly, allowing him to finally follow her in. Lying in just an inch or two of water, Jonas was able to finally rest his fingers. They were screaming in pain from the exertion he had put them through, but they had held him for the entire ordeal. Apparently even after five years on the bottle, he still had some measure of his previous strength and skill.

"As much as I wish we both had a moment to rest," Efigenia said, "I don't think we have the time for it. And I'm still not completely sure that the water in here is too shallow for a few piranhas to find their way in and start chewing us up."

The tunnel was almost completely dark and

smelled of ancient rotting plant matter. They didn't need to go that far down it before they found the path splitting in several directions.

"What even would this place be?" Jonas asked. "Do you have any ideas?"

"We obviously fell victim to a trap," Efigenia said, "but I doubt it would be the only one along the path. There are probably other piranha pits down the way from it. Whoever built and created Z would have needed a way to access the pits to both feed and replenish the fish."

"Which means there is likely some kind of maintenance entrance that would allow people to get in and out, or at least something that lets rainwater and trapped animals in to keep the piranhas alive for all this time."

It was difficult to tell time down in the dark, and once or twice Jonas thought he might have felt something nipping at his hands in the shallow water, although that could have just been his imagination. At one point they found themselves at the edge of another piranha pit, this one with a broken trapdoor near the top letting in a small amount of light, and they had to backtrack to a previous fork in order to try a different path. Not long after that, though, they came upon a vertical shaft with very intentionally carved hand and footholds in the stonework to form a sort of ladder. Given the extreme exhaustion of both of them, it took them longer to ascend then it might have otherwise, but they soon found themselves coming up through a hole in the ground and were back on the surface.

They were on an area high over the path like a watch or guard area, surrounded by broken rubble that might have very long ago been a building. The area was situated so that they might have been able to see the entire length of the road if the trees around them had been cleared. Looking down, Jonas could see the general area where they had fallen in. There was no sign anymore of the group from Graft-Horton.

“Let’s go back and see if they left our remaining pack behind,” Jonas said. “We’re going to need it if we’re going to survive out here.”

It was dark by the time they found a path back down to the initial trap. Both Jonas’s pack and the machete were still there, abandoned as not worth it by the Graft-Horton group.

Efigenia looked forlornly down the road where Graft and his people had gone. It would be too much to hope they had triggered another trapdoor by themselves, especially after the two of them had inadvertently revealed what the traps looked like. "They've got to be at least two hours ahead of us by now," she said dejectedly. "There's no way we can catch up in time."

Jonas opened up the pack and went through the supplies that were left. Thankfully they had put all the maps in this one when they'd packed up hurriedly this morning, but most of their food was gone. He stared at the map and tried to find where they likely were on it, as well as where he thought he might have originally lost the Carter expedition.

Finally he said, "Efigenia, I think we should go back."

She shook her head vehemently. "No. We have to keep going. I know it will be tough for us to do much out here with what little we have left, but we can't let them reach Z."

"No, I don't mean going all the way back to where we came from. I mean we have to backtrack and take a different route."

"But how would that help us? This is the direction that the stone wall said to go, unless we were reading it wrong."

"No, I think we were reading it correctly, but

I'm not sure anymore that we should completely trust that map. We already know there were changes to the landscape between then and now, but what if parts of the map were wrong on purpose?"

"Why would whoever built the city go to the trouble of carving a map to it in stone but intentionally get it all wrong? Especially since we can see right here that they built a road of some kind leading to it."

"Because maybe it wasn't actually supposed to lead people to the city. Maybe it was supposed to keep people away."

"Why would they want to build an entire city and then keep people away from it, though?"

"You're the professor," Jonas said. "I'll leave that speculation to you. But think about it. We followed the general direction the stone map said to go, and one of the first things we ran into was a kind of trap. I think it might have been a way to keep whoever they considered undesirable from reaching Z. I think the path we are currently on is either a misdirection or an intentionally circuitous route that could easily be watched and controlled."

Jonas pointed out a couple of specific places on

the map. "But the other thing you need to keep in mind is that if Carter was looking for Z, she didn't let me in on it at all, and I was the one doing the guiding. She was steering me in a sort of general direction, but we weren't following a marker or sign of any kind, just going by landmarks or her suggestions. And I think that, based on what I remember from that trip, there is a quicker way for us to get there if we ignore the directions from the stone map and instead go more directly to the west."

While Efigenia didn't appear too enthusiastic about this, neither did she look inclined to argue with him. "At this point we don't have anything to lose. But I'm not comfortable with this. Given a choice between a hunch and an actual map, I'd usually prefer to follow the map."

The part of Jonas that had spent the last five years hiding away in a bottle in his apartment wanted to stop fighting and just let her have her way. But there was a greater part of him left over from the life he had led before, the part that knew to trust his knowledge, experience, and instincts. He had been a respected guide for a long time, far longer than either he or the rest of the world had considered him a failure. "Your disapproval is noted, but irrelevant. You hired me to guide you and keep you safe, and that's what I'm going to keep doing, but I also swear to you, if you trust me, I'll get you to Z before Graft gets there. And if I don't, then you don't have to pay me for any of this."

Efigenia paused in thought for nearly a minute before she finally answered him. "Something tells me that I wouldn't even have the chance to not pay you, if it came down to that. If we don't get proof that Z exists and Graft is trying to destroy it, we likely will either mysteriously die in the rainforest at his request or we will get offed when we return. Our only chance is to try something they aren't. So we'll go your way."

They packed everything back up and immediately set to backtracking.

CHAPTER NINE

On the one hand, time was of the essence, but on the other, both of them were exhausted and in pain from the trials of the day. It was also night now, and trying to travel through the rainforest in the dark was a recipe for disaster. So the two of them hiked on for as long as their bodies could and there was any light at all, at which point they finally stopped for the night and made a half-assed attempt at a camp. There was just a little bit of food still available for them to eat, and they both took their fill of it. Jonas would likely be able to find things they could eat in their environment once the light was up again, but for now they needed anything at all that could help them recover. They started a fire but kept it small, as they needed something to keep animals away while still not attracting the attention of any Graft-Horton member that might still be within visual distance from them. Efigenia's bedroll was gone, so they shared one in completely platonic manner. Even if either of them had even wanted to engage in any sort of romantically-inclined activity, neither of them had the energy or stamina left for any such thing. Jonas reflexively woke several times in the night and patrolled the perimeter of their meager camp, but there was nothing that attracted his attention.

He woke her as soon as he detected even the slightest hint of the sky lightening, and with little conversation they packed up and started along again. Very soon after that, he started to get a distinct feeling of déjà vu as he looked at their surroundings. They might not have been on the exact same path that he had used five years earlier, but he felt like he remembered just enough to know that they were getting close to where he'd last seen Carter and the rest of her team. They stopped once just long enough to look at their maps, comparing where they likely were now to where, according to his best guess based on what they remembered from the way marker, the Graft-Horton group probably was. If they had lost a lot of their sense of urgency once they believed there was no longer a rival expedition looking for the same place, then there really was a decent chance that the two of them could reach the city first. He didn't want to chance it, though, so after a very short break they continued on.

It was late morning when Jonas once again told Efigenia to stop. There were some fruits nearby that would be safe for the two of them to eat, and as they did so Jonas surveyed their surroundings to make sure that initial thoughts upon stopping had been correct.

"This is it," he said. "That tree over there? I remember the odd shape the limbs are making. This is the place where we camped five years ago, and when I woke up in the morning Carter and her people were gone."

For the first time since the day before, Efigenia seemed to perk up. "So we're close? How long was it before you found our 'geological oddity?'"

"It was late in the day on the first day I went looking for them. I was following what I thought seemed like a trail from them, but it went cold. However, I don't think I picked up on that particular thread until after lunch. So the actual distance from here to there shouldn't be too far. Just give me some time to try to reorient myself."

He pulled out their maps again for consultation, and after looking around some more he pointed in direction to the northeast of their current position. "I think it's that way, but we'll need to remember this spot in case we need to come back and go a different direction."

That caution proved to be completely unwarranted. Within half an hour they came upon the long rock face that Jonas had originally believed to be a natural formation. In fact, he still would have believed that if he didn't know everything Efigenia had told him, at least from a distance. It wasn't until they were both practically against it that it became blindingly obvious that this had been created at some point by human hands.

"I guess I thought it would be grander than this," Efigenia said.

"There's probably almost a thousand years' worth of growth on top of it all," Jonas said. "If we could actually see all of it without that, I bet it would be spectacular."

To his trained eye, though, it was still a sight to behold. There shouldn't have been any sort of structure out here at all, so the presence of a wall taller than himself was impressive. And it was broken at the top with rubble at the bottom, implying that at one point it had been even taller. He pointed to the pack, which she had been carrying for the last hour or so of their journey.

"Can I see those satellite image maps you have?" he asked. She opened up her pack and handed him the images, which he compared to the map. "Look," he said. "See these enormous hills here? And here? The topographic map registers them as hills as well, but what if they aren't? Remember when you said that hills and mountains don't appear that quickly? Well, they could if they aren't really hills and mountains. I think your satellite images are actually showing the lost city of Z, it's just covered under a thousand years of dirt and plant life."

"That would make sense, I suppose," Efigenia said. "Most of the people who set out looking for the lost city of Z were expecting it to still be something beautiful and extravagant. You know, like people envisioned the golden city of El Dorado. No one was expecting it to be so totally reclaimed by the rainforest that no one would actually recognize it for being man-made at all when they saw it." She took the satellite maps back from him and stared at them herself. "Holy shit. If you're right, then this whole section of the map here would be the city. We've been staring directly at it and just thought it was part of the geology."

"How does it compare in size to that other site that people thought might be Z?" Jonas asked. "That Kuhikugu place?"

"It's not spread out quite as much, but if these formations we're seeing on the satellite images are indeed buildings instead of landforms? Then the architecture and structures here are far grander than anything in Kuhikugu. And I won't be able to tell further until we get inside the walls, but I'm already seeing some architectural elements that are completely unique and don't match other things from this region at all. I wouldn't call any of it Graeco-Roman in design like the manuscripts did, but if I squint I might be able to see how an uneducated eye might have got that confused."

"And does it still seem like something so much older than any other civilization that would be around here, or does it seem like something that fits into the currently understood history of the area?" Jonas asked.

"It's hard to tell from outside these walls. We'll have to get in to be sure, but I can tell you this much: one way or the other, this place is a significant archaeological find, and even if it's not the true Lost City of Z, it is still something we absolutely have to protect from Graft and his hoard of developers."

"There's got to be a way in," Jonas said. "I think when I originally saw this wall and didn't realize it was man-made, I went to the left and gave up soon after. If we go to the right, maybe we'll see something I missed last time."

"There's no telling how long the wall goes on for," Efigenia said. "If you're right about what the hills and landmasses in the satellite image actually are, then the city could be huge, and the wall could go around the entire thing."

"We would have to find an entrance eventually, right?" Jonas said. "There has to be more than one way in. Why would anyone build a city and then not leave ways to enter and exit?"

"We can't assume anything," Efigenia said. "We don't know what the purpose of this place might have been. Maybe it really was a city and would have multiple ways in and out. Or maybe it could have been a prison and entrances and exits would have been a liability. We just can't even begin to speculate until we get inside and get a better idea of the layout."

They started following along the outside of the wall. Jonas remembered going alongside it for at least an hour in the other direction, but he'd been looking for signs of human life then that were completely different than what they were trying to find now. They would stop every so often to check and investigate the wall further, just to be sure there weren't any signs or way markers along it that they were missing, but there was nothing even remotely like what they had originally found earlier. The wall did snake and turn in almost organic directions, though. It didn't just keep going on in a straight line, which had probably helped disguise it from him five years earlier as anything other than a natural part of the landscape. They did try to move swiftly, knowing full well that every extra moment it took them to find an entrance was an additional moment that Graft and his people would have to find this place and get in before them. They had to follow the wall for nearly another hour, and Jonas was starting to think that they might have missed something.

But when they did find the entrance, there was no mistaking it. This truly was it. This had to be the Lost City of Z.

CHAPTER TEN

Even with hundreds or thousands of years of weathering in the middle of the Brazilian rainforest, the arched entranceway to Z was something truly spectacular to behold. It rose roughly thirty or forty feet in the air and was twenty-five or so feet wide at the base, wide enough that two or three animal-drawn wagons or carts could go through it at a time. There was a bare patch immediately in front of the arch that suggested that, whatever traffic or force had gone through here hundreds or thousands of years ago, it had been enough that the ground was still unable to grow vegetation on it even after all this time.

Looking back in the direction that he assumed any such road would have come through, Jonas specifically kept his eye out for any sign that any other human or group may have been here recently. Rusty though he may be, he still had enough left of his old tracker's eye to know that no one had been through here recently. It really did look like they had managed to get here before Graft and his henchmen.

While time may have still been of the essence, Efigenia apparently couldn't keep that from overpowering her joy and wonder at the sight of the spectacular ruins. "Do you see this? *Do you see this, Jonas*? This sort of architecture has never previously been recorded in this region! This shouldn't be possible to make given what we know about the construction methods of the time, and it definitely shouldn't still be able to be standing, *and yet here it is*! It's real! Look! Look over there! Do you see that? That's clearly the remains of a door! They had doors that covered the whole front of this archway? Do you have any idea how…"

"Efigenia, calm down for a moment," Jonas said. "Or at least try to keep your voice low. It looks like we did in fact get here first, but we have no way of knowing how far behind they are. For all we know they could be just coming into earshot right now."

Efigenia's face fell and her eyes regained some of the worry and exhaustion they'd had earlier. "Right. Yes. I'm sorry, but you have to understand my excitement."

"I absolutely do, but the time to analyze all this from an archeological perspective is going to have to come later. Our own personal feelings about it…" Even as he said this, understanding dawned on him about what this meant for him and everything he had struggled with over the last five years. This had to be the answer to what had happened to Carter's team. Finally there would be closure. Except also, this meant that he had still messed up when he'd been searching for them. Just slightly more exploring in a different direction might have given him the answer he needed, and yet he had still missed it. In a way, this made him feel like an even bigger failure than he had felt like before.

No, I can't concentrate on that now, he thought. *That was five years ago. This is now. And right now I have this professor that needs my help and a group of well-funded murderers on their way to this exact spot at any moment. I have to focus on what's in front of me, not my past mistakes*.

"Our own personal feelings about any of this are just going to have to wait," he said. "For now we have an important question to ask: now that we've found Z, what do we do? How do we protect it against Graft?"

Efigenia's face fell. "I had some equipment that would have been able to reach some of my contacts on the outside. I had figured that all we would have to do is call them as soon as we saw the city, and that Graft wouldn't dare try anything while we were doing a live broadcast to the outside world. But all of that equipment was in the other pack."

"And I highly doubt the piranhas would be willing to give it back," Jonas said. He took a minute to think, and an idea occurred to him. It was a bit of a long shot, but it was all they had at the moment. "We have to find Carter."

"Jonas, I know you need closure, but there's no way they're still alive after all this time."

"I know that, but that's what I meant. When Carter and her people left me that morning, they took roughly half our gear with them. I brought back everything I could when I returned to civilization, and one thing that I know was not still there was their own satellite communication equipment. For days after I returned I kept hoping that there would be some signal from them letting me and the rest of the world know that they were still alive and needed extraction, but it never came. Wherever their bodies ended up, that gear has to still be with them. And with half our supplies gone, that gear is also probably the only way that you and I are going to get out of this forest, alive anyway. So we have to find it."

"Would it even still work after five years?"

"It's possible that it wouldn't, but most of it was sealed in weather-proof cases specifically to keep it from getting damaged in the region's heavy rains. If the gear didn't get taken out before they died, there's still a good chance that it would be useable."

"Then where do we start looking for them?" she asked.

Jonas pointed through the archway into the dark tunnel beyond it. "There's only one logical direction that they would have gone from here. Straight into Z."

They both stepped to just within the archway. The ground here was paved with heavy stones that were heaved up and uneven from the countless years of environmental changes, but it was still easy enough to walk on as long as they watched their step. The tunnel stretched on into darkness, making it difficult to see exactly how long it was. But the one thing they were able to see pretty quickly were the hundreds of extremely large spiders crawling on webs that crisscrossed the path.

"I'm no arachnologist," Efigenia whispered, "but I don't think it's even supposed to be possible for spiders to get that big."

"I saw camel spiders in Iraq that were kind of close to this, although I guess those aren't technically spiders," Jonas said. "Either they've got really abundant prey around here, or something in the environment allows them to grow this big." He thought about how big the anaconda they'd seen was, and also the size of the piranhas, and he thought that he might be on to something with that. But he wasn't a scientist. It wasn't his job to investigate that kind of thing. But in order to get the attention of someone who would look into it, they had to survive long enough to get back and report this info. "Either way, I'm thinking that neither of us want to be bitten by one."

That looked like it was going to be easier said than done, however. The whole passage was covered in webs, and the spiders languidly crawled around on them with no real care at the moment for the intruders staring at them. While he didn't want to get too close to any of them, they looked like they were possibly some variation of Brazilian Wandering Spiders, which would be a very bad thing for them if it was true. Wandering Spiders were considered to be among the top five most venomous spiders in the world, and while they still had some basic supplies left to deal with spider bites, he doubted that anything they had in their pack would save them if either of them were bitten by these things.

"We can either try finding another way into the city, or we can cut our way through this mess," Jonas said.

"I really, *really* want to say we should find some other way," Efigenia said, "but I don't think we have the time. Graft could be here at any time. If we don't go through here but they risk it and make it, then any advantage we have now will be lost."

"Then we're going to have to find some way to safely clear a path for ourselves," Jonas said. The corridor was very dark, lit only by what little light was spilling in from the entrance, so it seemed likely that the spiders could be anywhere on the walls, floor, and ceiling, hiding and waiting for prey just like them to come along. "I think we need torches, and I don't mean torches like the British refer to flashlights. I mean actual old-school low-tech flames on sticks."

"You know, it's funny," Efigenia said. "When I was gathering together the supplies for this expedition, there was a humorous moment where I thought about bringing a blowtorch. Doesn't seem like such a funny prospect now, though."

"Just as well," he said. "It would probably be swimming with the piranhas now."

They went back from the entrance to the main hall far enough that they were able to find some large, sturdy pieces of wood to use as the torch handles. They wrapped the tops with cloth and soaked the cloth in a small amount of kerosene they had for a lantern (even though the lantern itself was now gone), then lit the ends on fire. The torches wouldn't last long, but if they didn't dawdle they should last long enough to get them through the spider-infested corridor.

"Use the fire to scare away any spiders you see, and also to burn away any webs in front of you," Jonas said. "But don't move too quickly, or you might startle the spiders into attacking you."

"Very pleasant thought," Efigenia muttered, but she took the torch Jonas offered her and held it carefully and reverently. Together they went back into the entrance hall and slowly started to make their way down it. At first it wasn't easy to see how long the corridor went down for, but it wasn't long before Jonas thought he could see some kind of muted light at the end. Without the spiders, this wouldn't have been a worrying trek at all. But with them, a wrong move could prove deadly.

Every so often, the webs in front of them were thick enough that there was no way for either of them to maneuver around without disturbing them. In those cases they had to cautiously reach out with their torches and burn a path through without giving the spiders a cause to swarm them. Each web went up quickly like flash paper, but when a spider caught it burned for longer than Jonas would have expected, and gave out some kind of high-pitched screech as it died. Every time they did this, the other spiders seemed to grow more agitated.

And even as the spiders started to skitter closer and closer to them, the torches began to sputter as their limited fuel was running out.

"Jonas?" Efigenia asked. "I don't know if the torches are going to last all the way to the end of the hall."

"Speed up a little, but be careful," he responded. Rivulets of nervous sweat ran down his back, but he tried his hardest to keep his voice calm. The last thing Efigenia needed to know was that he was terrified.

As they approached the far end of the tunnel, Jonas could see that it split into two different directions. One remained wide enough for carts and wagons, while the other was smaller and seemed intended purely for foot traffic. It was here that the faint light had been coming from. Part of that exit was blocked off by fallen stonework, but there was still a large enough gap that they could get through one at a time. Jonas sent Efigenia through first, then, after making doubly sure that there were no spiders within striking distance of him, followed her through.

They found themselves in some kind of courtyard, but before Jonas could take any time to assess it, he realized that Efigenia was staring at something on the ground. There were skeletons just outside the entrance of the tunnel at their feet.

"I think we finally found them, Jonas," Efigenia said. "I think we've found Carter."

CHAPTER ELEVEN

There was no doubt that these were, in fact, the bodies of Arlene Carter and the rest of her people. There were four in all, one short of the total number that had gone missing, but it seemed possible that the fifth had either survived a bit longer than the others or had fallen prey to one of the hazards they'd encountered along the way to this specific spot. The skeletons were strewn about on the ground and their packs were ruptured and mostly reclaimed by the jungle, but some of the cases of equipment looked like they had managed to stay sealed against the elements. Jonas knew that he should check the equipment first and see if there was anything they could use, especially communication equipment, but he felt compelled instead by his past failure to investigate the skeletons first. There were still bits of old dead flesh on a few of them as well as bits of clothing that hadn't been natural enough for the local fauna to want to eat, but even with that it was hard to identify which body may have belonged to whom.

He thought back to his memories of that short time he'd spent with them, trying to bring back anything at all that could help him identify the individuals. He remembered that one of the assistants had worn a simple gold cross on a chain around his neck, and Carter herself had a sterling silver necklace with the shape of a compass rose. She'd said once that it was for when she "needed direction in her life." Another of the assistants had said he was married. Jonas found the skeleton with the wedding band first, then searched around the necks of the others. On the third one he found the gold cross. On the fourth he found the silver compass rose.

"That's it," Jonas said. "That's her."

"But what killed them?" Efigenia asked. "I don't see anything around them that implies violence or anything like that."

"Which would suggest to me that it was probably the spiders that did them in," Jonas said somberly. "I don't know if there's any way to know for sure anymore, though. The bodies are too decayed and eaten away."

"There's one person missing," she said. "You don't think it's possible they got away and somehow survived, do you?"

"If they went further into the ruins, I suppose it's possible if there's something in there we haven't seen yet that could sustain them, but I doubt it. If they tried to go back the way they came, they eventually would have likely run into me while I was searching for them. So I'm willing to bet we'll find at least one more body before we're done."

While Jonas continued to stare down at the bodies of the people he had been forced to leave behind five years ago, Efigenia looked around at their surroundings. Now that they were inside the walls, the Lost City of Z had quite the different look. The vegetation was still thick within the city after untold years of unchecked growth, but from this angle it now could definitely be recognized as a true city. There were clearly wide streets and thoroughfares beyond this mostly walled-off courtyard, and there were a number of buildings that could be seen some distance away - buildings that would have indeed looked like part of the landscape from above but from this angle were clearly man-made - that might have been upwards of five stories tall. In the more immediate vicinity, just within this courtyard, he thought he could see some spots that might have had buildings at one point but had collapsed due to time or the materials they'd been made from. At the end of this particular courtyard there was an arch leading into some large interior space, and it looked like they would have to go through it in order to reach most of the city.

Efigenia clearly had a hungry look in her eye like she wanted to start wandering around and investigate anything and everything, but before Jonas could try to get her back on track she slowly turned to him and, obviously pained at having to ignore the archeological wonder around them, asked him what they should do next.

Jonas indicated the cases. "We go through that and see if there's anything we can use, especially a way to call for help from the outside world."

"Is this really the best place to do that, though?" she asked. "Shouldn't we take it to some place in the ruins that's more hidden, just in case Graft arrives while we're trying to signal someone?"

"For our own safety, I think we need to get the message out sooner rather than later," Jonas said. "Did you already have someone waiting to hear from you?"

"Two people I know should be on standby

waiting for any word from me at all," Efigenia said. "My contact within the UN and a pilot with a helicopter in case we needed some kind of emergency extraction."

"Then I'll let you set up the equipment. You're the one who knows the channels to contact, and you would have more aptitude with the comm equipment than I would."

They started opening cases, and while Efigenia got to work assembling the comm equipment, Jonas went through everything else to see what they could use for survival. All the while, he kept a close eye and ear on the hall through which they had come, both to make sure that no spiders scuttled out and bit them when they weren't looking, and to be aware of any signs that they soon wouldn't be alone.

Jonas hadn't gotten very far into his inspection of the cases, finding so far only a few rations that weren't spoiled that they could use if they had to, when Efigenia started cursing quietly under her breath in a couple of different languages.

"What is it?" he asked.

"I think this might take me a lot longer than I initially thought," she said. "I knew pretty well how to operate the equipment that I'd brought with me, but there's just enough differences between that and what Carter brought that I'm having some trouble. This stuff is a lot bulkier, and I think it must have already been pretty old by the time Carter brought it out here."

"Do you still think you can use it? Or is it a lost cause?"

"No, I think I can still make it work. I just don't see any way that I could get it set up and broadcasting in less than an hour."

"Shit," he said. Jonas again turned his attention back briefly to the tunnel. At first there was nothing, but then he thought he could hear some faint voices from far away. There was no telling how long it would take them to get to this exact spot, especially with the dark hall and spiders in the way, but there was no doubt that Graft and his people had finally seen the entrance to Z.

"We're out of time," he said. "Quick, pack everything back in the cases, and then let's see what we can do about hiding them out of the way. They're too bulky for us to be able to bring them with us as we try to get out of Graft's way, so the best we can hope is that they don't see these cases so they're still here waiting for us when we have the ability to circle back to them."

"But what are we going to do to stop Graft once they're in the city?" Efigenia asked.

"I have no clue. We'll have to come up with that plan while we're running. We still have the advantage of them thinking that we're dead, so maybe we can set something up against them."

They packed up the equipment and pulled the stuff they considered important off to the side behind some rubble, but left some with the skeletons of Carter's team so that it didn't look too suspicious that some of it was missing. They then did their best to hide any sign that they had been there. It hurt Jonas that he had to leave the bodies to continue to lay out in the elements, but it would give them away to cover the bodies or do anything else for them as a sign of respect. He silently made a promise in his head that he would survive long enough to make sure Carter and the others received a proper burial, then started toward the far end of the courtyard and the archway into the extremely large building beyond.

Before either of them even stepped through the door, something in Jonas's instincts started going off in warning. He grabbed Efigenia by the shoulder before she could walk through.

"What's wrong?" she asked him.

"I don't really know," he said. "But something isn't right here."

"Do you just have the willies, or do you actually see some evidence that there's a problem? Because we don't have time to wait."

Indeed, it was very easy to now hear Graft's group coming through the main hall. Efigenia's joking reference earlier to a flame-thrower turned out to be prophetic, as it sounded like that was exactly what Graft's group was using to clear the spiders. It was too much to hope that one of the spiders would get through and take any of them out of the picture, but Jonas had hoped the arachnids would have at least slowed them down longer than this. Apparently, when you were the majority owner of a multi-billion-dollar corporation, you could afford to outfit your expedition with any and every piece of equipment that money could buy, right along with the people needed to haul it.

Jonas tried to count the number of people he heard in the hall. One of them sounded like that Schultz guy that had betrayed Efigenia, and it sounded like there were at least three other voices. Graft's voice wasn't among them, but there was no way he wasn't here after that long trek. So there were at least five people coming up on them soon, maybe more, and all of them would be ready to do something drastic as soon as they saw Jonas and Efigenia standing here.

He looked around the courtyard once more, searching for any other way out of here that didn't involve going through the large, ominous room ahead of them that didn't appear to have any notable purpose. There wasn't any. It occurred to him now why this had set his instincts off. The design of this area and the courtyard made it feel like they were being funneled toward something.

"There's traps ahead," Jonas muttered.

"That's crazy," Efigenia said. "This isn't a movie. In real life archaeological sites aren't riddled with traps."

"Except we already know that whoever designed Z was willing to do exactly that on the path that led here."

"Uh, yeah. You're right. But we can't stay here."

"You're right. We can't. So there's only one thing we can do."

He looked once more into the ominous room. "We are going to need to watch our step."

CHAPTER TWELVE

That was exactly what they both did as they first entered the room. Jonas made sure there was nothing particularly worrisome on the floor immediately within the door, and then took a moment to examine the room. Maybe it was a moment they couldn't afford, with the group that was about to stumble upon them at any minute, but Jonas's instincts were still screaming, and he had a feeling that it could be a possible death sentence for them both if he didn't listen to them.

If Jonas had to compare the size of the room to anything, he would say that the closest modern equivalent was an Olympic-size swimming pool. The walls on all sides went up about fifteen feet high, and there were small slits of windows near the top, enough to let light in and make sure the room wasn't completely dark, but also far too high up and small for any human to try getting out of the room through them. The only other way in or out of the room was on the very far side, further cementing the idea in his head that this was a room that not all people were intended to get out of.

Both the floor and the ceiling, he noticed, consisted of probably two hundred or so each of square stone tiles that were roughly three feet wide. These probably would have been the dominant feature in the room, except for some reason that wasn't immediately apparent as there was a single solid pillar of stone roughly two thirds of the way through the room and slightly off to the right. It was the same width as the tiles and connected one on the floor directly to the corresponding square space on the ceiling. The pillar didn't appear to be load-bearing in any way; it was just a random pillar at an odd placement in an otherwise empty room.

Behind them, voices could clearly be heard in the courtyard now. They were out of time. Jonas motioned for Efigenia to get out of sight from the courtyard, with her moving gingerly to one side of the door while Jonas did the same on the other side. They couldn't help but step on the tiles, but thankfully, for the moment, nothing happened.

It occurred to Jonas that Graft and his crew probably wouldn't enter this room with the same care that they had. If there were indeed traps in here, then it might be advantageous (if horrifying) to let their pursuers blindly stumble in and take the brunt of whatever traps there were here. He would just have to hope that those same traps didn't also happen to take out him and Efigenia with them. He gestured for Efigenia to be quiet, and then did his best to blend in with the shadows of his corner without actually moving from his spot.

The voices came closer. He could hear members of the group speculating about where they should go from here, but he couldn't help but notice that none of them seemed to have the same academic curiosity about this lost city that had sent Efigenia to chattering. Not one of them seemed to care that they were in an architectural and historical marvel. At least that lack of basic curiosity seemed to imply that they weren't going to bother taking any time to investigate the skeletons and their gear.

Thinking of the remains of Carter's team, Jonas remembered that a single member of that group had been missing from the bodies. That thought tickled some part of his brain, trying to make him solve a puzzle, and he found himself looking once again at the peculiar pillar that didn't seem to have any purpose in this room. Now that he was paying closer attention to the area around its base, he saw something poking out from one side that might have been the bones of a hand.

Suddenly he knew the purpose of the pillar, as well as what had happened to the final member of Carter's team.

Before he could try drawing Efigenia's attention to this fact, the first member of Graft's team walked through the door, and Jonas stood stock still, hoping the man wouldn't notice the two figures in the shadowed corners. Unlike Jonas, this man walked right through the door with no sense of caution whatsoever, and Jonas held his breath as he stepped on the first of several floor tiles. Nothing happened, but Jonas knew it was only a matter of time. Part of him wanted to be heroic and shout a warning to the man, but Graft's people had already tried to kill them at least once. If Jonas warned anyone, he would only be putting himself and Efigenia in danger.

Right behind the man, four other people followed. The narrow width of the door forced them to come through in a tight single file line immediately following the first man. Two of them were completely unknown to Jonas, but the remaining two were Schultz and Graft. Graft was in the very rear. Whether intentionally or not, he was letting all his cronies go first to take the brunt of any possible dangers that appeared before them.

Out of the entire team, the first four people in the room walked confidently like they were unworried. Only Graft hesitated. It was this hesitation that led him to look around once he was through the door, making him the first to realize they were not alone here.

"You!" he yelled as he saw Efigenia. The other team members were startled as Graft pulled a gun from inside his coat. At first Jonas almost believed it might be the same gun Efigenia had lost on the path, but this one, while it was the same type and caliber, had a different colored handle. "I should have shot you when I saw you hanging in that pit!"

Efigenia looked like she was about to dodge out of harm's way, and Jonas realized that she hadn't realized yet like he had the exact nature of the danger hidden in this room. In her panic she might get off her current spot and blunder onto one of the danger tiles. Although he wasn't sure that it was going to do them any good, Jonas screamed out at Graft before he could finish pointing the gun at her.

"Hey you, pick on someone your own size!" he yelled. It might have been lame, far from the pithy one-liners of a movie action hero that might be in his same situation, but he quite frankly didn't give a rat's ass about how clever he sounded at the moment. He just hoped that he could distract Graft for a few seconds in the hope that something else would happen.

And something else did, indeed, happen.

While Graft spun around in the direction of Jonas's voice, trying to bring the gun to bear along with him, his arm smacked into Schultz from behind. Schultz, completely confused by the sudden flurry of sound and movement behind him, stumbled off to the side several steps from Graft. Jonas saw the moment that his foot hit one of the hidden trap tiles.

The tile shifted slightly with a small puff of dust, and there was a horrid groan of stone on stone as some mechanism underneath him was triggered. Following his hunch, Jonas looked up to the ceiling immediately over him just in time to see the corresponding ceiling tile crack and break. A single stone pillar, just like the one that had already been present in the room, fell through the hole into the room below.

The enormous stone pillar slammed down on Schultz, splashing blood and viscera in a gruesome supernova pattern at its base. Immediately one of the other team members screamed and tried to run, blindly stepping on some other trick tile to cause another pillar to slam down on him. This one only caught the lower half of him, however, leaving the man half crushed and begging for help from a blood-covered mouth until he mercifully died ten seconds later.

After that, everyone remaining was smart enough to stand still.

There was a long moment of complete quiet in the room as everyone, completely stunned by what they had just seen, took a moment to comprehend what all this meant. Despite his heart hammering in his chest, Jonas kept his head enough to look around at the remaining members of Graft's team to assess how much of a threat they were. Everyone except Graft himself was carrying packs full of gear. One of the remaining people held the flame-thrower with a small tank of fuel on his back, but he looked tired and worn out from carrying the additional gear that no one else was expected to. The man who had been half crushed by the pillar had held a machete, which had slid from his hands and was now not that far away from Jonas. The remaining member of their team had a shotgun in hand, but he appeared to be too stunned by what had just happened to think about pointing it at either Jonas or Efigenia. Graft still had his revolver ready, but he didn't point it anywhere in particular.

Jonas also took a look at the pack of the man who'd had his lower half crushed. It had opened when he'd fallen and a number of items had fallen out of it, but either they hadn't landed on any of the pressure tiles or they weren't heavy enough to trigger a pillar. While Jonas didn't know too much about explosives, he saw a wrapped block of what looked like gray clay among the debris. That would be C4, he assumed. That was what they were going to use to destroy the city. As far as he knew, the impact of the falling pillars alone wouldn't be enough to set off the explosives if it came to that, as he believed C4 would only go off with a special trigger. However, he wasn't completely certain of that, so he didn't want to be anywhere nearby if any of the other team members were also carrying it and subsequently got squished.

Although Jonas would have preferred not to speak to their rivals at all, he still figured he had to take the chance. “Graft, I don’t suppose you know how to get through this, do you?” Jonas called to him.

“If I did I certainly wouldn’t tell you,” Graft called back.

“Fucking hell, Graft, we’re all in this together,” Efigenia said.

“Not the way I see it,” Graft said back. “I’m not going to give up on billions of dollars of real estate investment just because you two want to protect some moldy old Aztec pyramids.”

Efigenia looked at Jonas. “I really don’t understand why someone hasn’t already killed this guy,” she said.

“Money,” Jonas muttered. “It can’t make people like you, but it can make people protect you against everyone you’ve ever screwed over.”

For several moments no one moved or said anything. Jonas looked up at the ceiling above them, trying to find any indication of which of the ceiling tiles actually hid the giant crushing pillars, but if there had been some sign at one point, those signs had been worn away by age. He checked the floor for the same thing, and found it similarly worn and overgrown. The tiles that he could still see, though, reminded him of something he'd seen recently. Making sure that he didn't move at all from his current spot, Jonas carefully removed his pack, opened it, and then rummaged through it until he found the tracings he'd made back when they had found the stone way marker. He had to reorient them several times to make sure he was looking at them the right way, but eventually he satisfied himself that the checkerboard pattern did in fact seem to correspond to the faint and faded markings on the stone at their feet. His initial thought was that the tracing was a map showing the location of the deadly pillars, but the more he looked the more he realized that couldn't be right. All three of the pillars that had slammed down seemed to be in positions that the map would have indicated as safe.

"That doesn't… wait," Jonas said. "Maybe that does make sense."

"Talk to me, Jonas," Efigenia said. "Please tell me you have a way for us to get out of here."

"Maybe," Jonas said. He carefully leaned down and reached out to grab the machete near him on the ground. Keeping the machete might be helpful, while losing it could cause them problems later, but for now Jonas had more pressing concerns, possibly literally. He looked at the tracing one more time, then gingerly reached out with the end of the machete to one of the tiles next to him and pressed down on it with the tip, making sure his actual hand wasn't over the tile just in case his theory was wrong.

Nothing happened. No pillar came crashing down to smash the end of the machete. He whooped in triumph and looked around at the others. No one, not even Efigenia, seemed to realize what he'd just discovered. He stepped to the tile he'd just tested, looked at the tracing again, and found another tile that would work. Although he was reasonably certain he'd found the answer, he tested this one as well with the machete's end. Still no instant death. He stepped onto the tile, this time with a lot more confidence that it wouldn't kill him.

The markings on the way marker had been made to look like they showed which tiles were safe, but that had been yet another trap. By *avoiding* the spots that the tracing seemed to imply were okay, he would be able to navigate the tiles and come out safely on the other side. He realized, however, that he would have to be careful how he indicated this to Efigenia. He wanted her to make it to safety with him, but it was in their best interest for Graft and his people to still not know exactly what was happening. He started calling out instructions to her, but he made sure she avoided when possible any tiles that brought either of them alongside Graft's people. They would know which spots were safe by where the two of them stepped, but they wouldn't know whether the spots between were safe or if they were deathtraps.

As soon as Graft realized what he was doing, he yelled to Jonas. "Drammond, I will pay you an obscene amount of money if you tell me how to escape this with you."

"Graft, you have got to be kidding me. You've already attempted or threatened to kill us multiple times, even after I myself suggested we work together," Jonas said. "I have zero reason to trust a single thing you say, even if you did somehow find some amount of money that would get me to turn to you and away from the client that I'm already serving. Which, by the way, would be far more money than even you will possibly make in your entire life."

Both Jonas and Efigenia were over halfway through the room by the time that Graft remembered the gun in his hand. He pointed it at Jonas, but Jonas didn't allow himself to flinch. "I'm warning you, Drammond. Tell me how to get out of this or I will shoot you both."

"If you do that, you definitely won't find out what I know," Jonas said. "If I were you, I would stop using your concentration to threaten me and instead try to memorize the steps we're taking so you can follow us."

Graft looked down at the tiles at Jonas and Efigenia's feet. It obviously hadn't occurred to him before that he should have been doing that from the beginning. Graft may have been horrifically rich, but he sure hadn't earned any of that money through his own smarts.

Graft started to frantically command his two remaining people. As he did this, both Jonas and Efigenia reached the far door. Without any further look back, both of them walked out back into the open sunlight, and finally onto the proper thoroughfares of the lost city known as Z.

CHAPTER THIRTEEN

Their first immediate concern was to get as far away from Graft and the trap room as they possibly could. Jonas continued to watch their step and they ran for a large and squat building nearby, but he didn't think it would make sense for the general open areas to have any traps. Whatever the purpose had been for Z to begin with, it still would have needed to function in that purpose, so whoever had built it wouldn't just put traps willy-nilly all over it. Within some of these buildings it might be different, but he felt mostly safe as long as they stayed outside. Mostly. He still planned to be overly cautious whenever he could.

Once they were both out of sight of the trap room's exit, they took the briefest of moments to rest and catch their breaths. "Are you okay?" Jonas asked her.

"Yes. I'm fine," she said. "I'm completely…" In mid-sentence she hunched over and threw up her meager breakfast on the stonework of the ground. She dry heaved a few times, then wiped her mouth with her forearm. "Er, sorry. It's just… what happened to Schultz and that other guy, the way he just splattered…"

Jonas patted her back and assured her it was okay. Probably both of them would come out of this with some level of post-traumatic stress disorder, so he certainly wasn't going to hold her vomiting against her. Jonas, for his part, thought he could compartmentalize those gruesome images from his active mind until after they were out of here and back to safety.

However, as long as Graft was still here and intent on destroying Z, they had to assume that any safety they found was temporary. With that thought, Jonas felt there was something he had to address. "Maybe we should address the elephant in the room. Graft has tried to kill us. If he finds us, he will try again. But right now, Graft and his remaining people are in a prone position. The smartest thing to do right now might actually be to go back and trigger some of those traps to take them out. It would probably be considered self-defense."

Efigenia looked like she was going to be sick again at that concept, but she did at least take half a minute of silence to consider it. “No. We can’t. We’re not him. If there’s a way for us to get out of this alive while still being able to take him back to civilization to face justice for everything he’s done, we’ve got to try for it, all the way up until we truly have no other choice.”

Jonas nodded. Personally, he wouldn’t have lost too much more sleep than he already had if they went back right now and made sure Graft never left that room. He truly would feel that it was self-defense. But he was for hire here, and his client had said no. Regardless of whether or not he thought it was the smart move, he would follow her lead and abide by her decision.

“Then we have until they figure out how to get onto our tiles and remember our routes out to come up with a plan,” he said. “Unless we find some other way out of the walls, the only way to reach the comm equipment is by going back through that room. Now, it didn’t occur to any of those idiots that if we weren’t going to help them then there was no reason not to shoot us, but they might finally realize that if we try to backtrack and go right past them, so that’s out of the question.”

“They weren’t so far in that they couldn’t have

found their way back out where we all came from though, right?" Efigenia asked. "They could backtrack out to the outer wall again and look for another way into the city."

"If there even is another way in, it would take them far too long to find it," Jonas said. "If I had to guess what Graft is going to try doing, he's going to have his two henchmen try to brute force their way through on the general paths he saw us taking. They might not make it through, but he won't care. So we need to figure out what they would try to do once they're through."

"Well, Graft wants to destroy this place, at least enough that no one would realize it had been here until after the entire thing is bulldozed," Efigenia said. "They will have explosives with them, but I don't know what kind."

"I saw it spill out of the pack of the man that got killed," he said. "It was C4. And it wasn't like they were carrying enough to simply wire every building in this city."

Indeed, now that they had a chance to examine their surroundings, it was quite evident that such a thing was impossible. The city was huge, bigger than he could possibly have expected. There were quite a few buildings still standing, and just as many in a partial state of disrepair. There could have been a lot more than even they were seeing, since the jungle growth had made its way in and covered any number of things. Part of Jonas wanted to speculate on what Z was and why it was here, possibly who had built it, as it didn't look like any other culture that he'd ever seen evidence of in this region. But he wasn't the historian here, and speculating about that kind of thing wasn't his job.

"They would be looking for some place where one or a few key explosions could do something to the rest of the city," Jonas said. "We need to explore at least enough to figure out where that might be."

They pulled out their maps and did their best to locate their current location, although such a thing was extremely difficult. Jonas did think he saw something interesting, however, and he got them walking in the general direction of some higher ground. Soon enough, they found themselves starting to go up a hill that seemed to be real, rather than just a building covered in dirt and growth. The hill was almost a mountain, really, and probably would have worked very well as some kind of watch tower back in the days when people actually lived or worked here. This was probably exactly the place they needed to find.

"Right there," Jonas said, gesturing from a spot on the map to a place on the hill about a quarter mile up from them. "If I were them, that's where I would try to plant the explosives."

"How can you be so sure?" Efigenia asked.

"I can't be," he said. "But if they want to destroy the entire site with as minimal effort as possible, and maybe even make it look natural in the process, then just blowing everything up wouldn't do. But if they put the bomb in just the right place, well, just look at those cliffs. They're supporting a lot of the rocks and growth of the mountain. Blow up the cliffs, and all of that will come tumbling down with enough mass and force to destroy most of the city. Probably something future people here will want to shore up to protect the site."

"If there even are any future people here that aren't living in a condo," Efigenia said. She looked back down the path they had come. They were starting to rise above many of the trees now, giving them a slightly better view of the lost city spread out behind them. "We haven't even had the chance to explore what might be down there.

There could be things that could convince Graft to stand down if we knew about them."

"The city could be the location of the Holy Grail, the lost Ark of the Covenant, hidden Nazi treasure, and the body of Jimmy Hoffa, and I still don't think it would sway Graft," Jonas said. "People like him don't have any sense of history and what came before, just the now and what comes in the future. You could argue with him until you're blue in the face and he wouldn't hear any of it."

"Do you think we can get to that spot before Graft does?" she asked.

"Assuming they get out of that room, yes. He's lost most of his crew," Jonas said. "And a billionaire like that probably isn't particularly practiced in traipsing around through the jungle. If we move quickly, I think it's possible."

While the growing incline was grueling, neither of them complained as Jonas set a brisk pace up the side of the mountain. While time was certainly of the essence, Jonas couldn't help but look back every so often as the Lost City of Z fell farther and farther below them. Efigenia did the same, and as the archeologist between the two of them, she was the one who was most in danger of getting distracted by the sight.

"From here it's even more Graeco-Roman looking than it was at ground level. I can see why the writers of the two manuscripts would think…"

"Efigenia, I understand that analyzing it is like breathing to you, but now is really not the time," Jonas said. "If we stop Graft, you'll have plenty of time afterward to investigate to your heart's content."

"But I still have to make observations," she said. "If Graft does succeed and he destroys this place, my account will be the only modern one documenting that this place ever existed at all."

"If Graft succeeds, it will probably kill us right along with the city, and it won't matter whether or not you've observed anything at all here."

"Oh. Right. Good point," she said sheepishly.

As they approached the point he had indicated, Jonas paid more and more attention to any sounds or signs that they might not be alone on the steep mountainside. While they'd been working under the assumption that Graft was still behind them, they couldn't know that for sure, just as they couldn't know that he wouldn't have found a route to get here quicker than them. There was less plant cover the higher and steeper they went up, but there would still be enough that someone could hide among it. Jonas thought it unlikely that Graft himself would have enough experience to get here without them seeing him, but maybe his remaining team members would be able to do it.

"Hey, Efigenia, would I be correct in assuming someone like Graft doesn't have any field or tracking experience?" Jonas asked.

"You would think so, but it's possible he might," she said. "I know that he got his fortune from a family diamond mine in Africa, so maybe he's got some experience in the bush. It probably would not be the best idea to just assume that he's never been out from behind a desk for his entire life."

"You would assume right about that," someone said from the slope just above them. They both looked up, and on the ledge that Jonas had indicated, Graft was already standing there, looking at them both and pointing his gun at them.

CHAPTER FOURTEEN

In the moments that Graft stood there over them gloating, Jonas assessed the situation and their environment. The steeper the mountainside had become, the less vegetation there was, and in their immediate position there wasn't much of anything around them. There seemed to be quite a bit up on the cliff ledge surrounding Graft, however, and there was enough below and around them that maybe someone could sneak through it to get up to Graft. In Jonas's mind, a plan started to form.

Graft disappeared for just a few seconds from the side of the cliff like he was checking something. It was enough that Jonas could whisper instructions to Efigenia.

"Hit me like you're betraying and leaving me, take the machete, and disappear into the brush below," he said to her.

"Why?" she asked. "What would…"

"Just do as I say, then while he's distracted by me find a way up through the brush and sneak up behind him. No time for any questions. Hit me.

Now!"

Even though he had told her to do it, the sucker punch she landed to his face set his ears to ringing, and it wasn't hard at all to sell the idea that she'd got him good. Up above he could hear Graft coming back to the edge at the commotion she was causing. Right as she grabbed the machete out of his hand, Graft's gun went off and a bullet hit the dirt near his leg. He didn't know if it was intended as a warning shot or if he was just a terrible aim, but he didn't want him to have another chance to fire before she was gone. He pushed her like he was fighting back against her, and she tumbled down the slope and vanished from view into the bushes. All he could do was hope that she hadn't hurt herself for real in the fall.

"Stop moving, or I won't miss next time," Graft said down to him. "I'm going to watch you very carefully and let you climb up just enough to get your footing, but don't try anything. If you do I'm going to shoot you in the head."

Without saying anything, Jonas slowly and carefully did exactly as he was told. When he finally crawled up on the ledge with Graft, he moved to stand up, but Graft gestured for him to stay in a kneeling position.

"You mind telling me what exactly that was that just happened?" Graft asked.

"She's been acting weird ever since you left us in that pit," Jonas said. "Can't seem to figure out whether she wanted to keep going or turn back. I guess as soon as she saw you standing over us with a gun again she decided she didn't want to mess with it anymore."

"Hmm. You'll understand if I don't exactly believe you," Graft said. "I know a little about you, but I know far more about her. She's not going to just leave and let me have this place. She's too stubborn and selfish for that. Either you both have something planned, or she decided to try something without consulting you."

While Graft believed that he had the upper hand, Jonas took a second to look around at the state of the flat area of ledge they were on. There were trees and plants immediately surrounding them, but above this area there was nothing but rocky mountainside. There was no sign of the two other men they'd left Graft with in the trap room, but there was in fact a bomb set up nearby. There seemed to be a timer on it, but it wasn't facing in a direction where he could see for certain. It looked like his earlier assessment had been right. Graft was indeed expecting a landslide from the mountain to come down and bury most of the city. It might not bury all of it, but all Graft really needed was to hide the city for a little longer until he got his developers in here.

"What happened to your men?" Jonas asked.

Graft's expression hardened into a grimace. "They didn't make it out of there. But they set off just enough of those pillar traps on their way to the other side that I was able to figure out the path I needed. And now all I need to do is take you out, then wait for your companion to try to come back."

"What exactly are you planning to do, Graft?" Jonas asked. "Stand here and guard the bomb until it explodes?"

For a moment Graft finally started to look worried. He recovered quickly, but Jonas made note that the man could still be shaken. "Maybe you can figure out how to disarm it, but I doubt she could. If I shoot you, it won't matter if she comes back. The bomb will go off, I'll be gone, and the developers can come in."

"Graft, listen to me," Jonas said. He saw some subtle movement in the brush behind Graft, but he did his best not to react to it. "Do you even understand what you're going to be destroying here? There's history here that can never be replaced, knowledge about civilizations that we know nothing about." Jonas tried to sound as sincere as possible in his words, like maybe he really thought he could convince the man, but he knew Graft would never be swayed by such arguments. Behind Graft, some of the bushes slowly and gently parted, revealing Efigenia sneaking up from behind with the machete. She was moving incredibly slowly so as not to cause any foliage to rustle, and there was a lot of space between her and Graft, so Jonas had to keep the man from glancing in that direction for as long as possible.

"All of that history, as you call it, is completely worthless to the modern world," Graft said. "No one really cares about moldy old ruins. They certainly say they do, but that's just so they can make themselves look better to the public around them. A hundred years from now, no one will even care what was or wasn't here before. This land can be put to much better use if some United Nations council isn't telling people like me what we can and can't do with it just because it has a bunch of toppling old buildings on the site."

Yeah, that's right, just keep monologuing, Jonas thought. Efigenia was closer, but Jonas could see that she was hesitant about using the machete on an actual human rather than on underbrush. While she had done some field work in the past, she had likely never encountered a situation where she might need to harm another person to ensure her own survival. It was unfortunate that their roles weren't reversed, as Jonas believed he could take down Graft with minimal damage to his conscience. But despite any field experience she may have had, she was inherently a book worm, and Jonas doubted she had ever had to resort to true violence ever in her life.

"Just think about that for a second," Jonas started to say. "That kind of…"

Efigenia stepped on some branch that snapped loudly beneath her. Graft spun around with the gun to aim it in her direction, and at the same moment Jonas rushed him. Efigenia tried to duck as Graft fired the pistol, holding up the machete in front of her as though she hoped it could act as a shield. Amazingly it worked, and the bullet ricocheted off into the jungle, but the force from the impact sent the machete flying out of her hands and tumbling down the mountainside. Jonas hit him, and the two of them fell to the ground right at the edge of the cliff. The gun flew out of Graft's hands and skidded over to a halt near Efigenia. She immediately grabbed it and pointed it at Graft as he wound up for a punch to Jonas's face.

"Stop!" she yelled at him. "This is all over. If you try to do anything else to us, I'll shoot!"

"Go ahead, shoot," Graft said. "See if I care." He smashed Jonas in the face and pushed him closer to the edge. One more good hit or shove, and Graft would send him tumbling over the side. The slope a few feet under the ledge might have been enough to break Jonas's fall if he went over, but it was just as possible that Jonas could hit it wrong and break his neck.

Graft made a move like he was about to shove Jonas over the edge. Efigenia pulled the trigger and fired.

Nothing happened.

Graft sneered at her. "I used three of the bullets before we got here this morning on some creature chasing us in the forest. And then I used the last one to put one of my men out of his misery when one of those pillars only partially got him. That thing's useless without the extra bullets I've got in my pockets."

He turned back to Jonas and punched him a few more times. Jonas felt himself approaching the edge of a blackout as Graft pushed him all the way to the very edge of the cliff.

"Now if you'll excuse me," he said to Jonas. "I need to get rid of you while I still have enough time to get…"

The gun went off, and Graft's head exploded as a bullet went through it.

Jonas pushed Graft off of him, sending the body tumbling down the side. He looked up at Efigenia and had to blink several times to clear his head.

"How…?" he asked. "How could you shoot without bullets?"

"He wasn't the only one with bullets in his pocket this whole time, remember?"

Jonas wanted to comment on that, maybe even laugh in the maniacal way of someone who has to do so in the face overwhelming trauma, but he suddenly remembered they were still very much in danger. "The bomb! We have to disarm it."

"Do you even know how?"

"No, but we have to try. If we don't… wait."

Jonas had run over to the bomb, but once he saw the timer, he stopped. Efigenia came up next to him and they both stared at the digital readout on the trigger.

It wasn't even on.

"Did… did he forget to set it?" Efigenia asked.

"Maybe," Jonas said. "But more likely… I don't think he even knew how to use it. Without any of his people, he was completely at a loss to do anything at all."

They stared at the useless bomb for several moments. Then, finally, they allowed the laughter to come.

CHAPTER FIFTEEN

The first thing they had to do was go back to the comm equipment. Efigenia tried to set it up, but found that in their current position the signal was either too weak or it was being blocked by some feature of the city itself. With several hours of painstaking, nerve-wracking work, they maneuvered the equipment cases through the trap room, then back to the mountain and finally set it up on the ledge where they had fought Graft. Here, finally, they were able to get it to work, and Efigenia was able to reach her contact with the helicopter. It was then a matter of a couple more hours while they waited for rescue. Both of them ate some of the rations and slept, and soon after Jonas woke from his nap, he saw something coming in the air.

"Look, there it is!" Jonas said, pointing at a spot near the horizon. "I'm glad that the comm equipment still worked. When Carter bought equipment, she apparently bought stuff that would last no matter how old it already was."

A small dot was soaring over the rainforest, and as it slowly got bigger they could both hear the increasing noise of helicopter propellers.

However, Efigenia didn't seem that interested at the moment in their imminent rescue. Instead she was staring at Jonas with an intense curiosity. "Is this going to change anything for you?" she asked.

Jonas thought about it for a long moment, then nodded. "What happened to Carter and her team wasn't my fault. I realize that now. And with the remains of her journal that I found in her equipment, I can prove it to the rest of the world, too, if anyone tries to blame me. And even if she did just abandon me in the jungle, I still feel obligated to bring what we can of her and the others back to their families so they can get closure."

"We can make sure that the bodies are retrieved after we've gotten back to my university and we can alert the proper authorities of everything that happened here," Efigenia said.

"And what are your plans?" Jonas asked. "Other than the obvious research base operations you're going to need to set up to study Z?"

"Well, it's not just going to be about preserving

Z. It's going to be about keeping the entire region safe from people like Graft in the future. And keeping the people and tribes here safe as well. That includes the displaced tribe we met on the way here, as well as anyone else living out here that we may not have met yet. This whole area needs to be protected from the future Grafts that would come for it."

The helicopter was close enough now that it seemed to see them when they waved their hands in the air to catch its attention. There wasn't an immediate area where the vehicle could land, but as it approached Jonas could see someone getting a rope ladder ready to throw out the side. Jonas checked the vehicle for any signs that it might actually be associated with Graft-Horton, but it seemed to just be a standard rescue chopper. He had Efigenia climb the ladder first, then went up himself.

As Jonas took one last look out over the Lost City of Z, it occurred to him that he hadn't craved a drink in some time. He nodded quietly to himself.

Time to start prepping for the next adventure, he thought.

Check out other great

Cryptid Novels!

Hunter Shea

LOCH NESS REVENGE

Deep in the murky waters of Loch Ness, the creature known as Nessie has returned. Twins Natalie and Austin McQueen watched in horror as their parents were devoured by the world's most infamous lake monster. Two decades later, it's their turn to hunt the legend. But what lurks in the Loch is not what they expected. Nessie is devouring everything in and around the Loch, and it's not alone. Hell has come to the Scottish Highlands. In a fierce battle between man and monster, the world may never be the same. Praise for THEY RISE : "Outrageous, balls to the wall...made me yearn for 3D glasses and a tub of popcorn, extra butter!" – The Eyes of Madness "A fast-paced, gore-heavy splatter fest of sharksploitation." The Werd "A rocket paced horror story. I enjoyed the hell out of this book." Shotgun Logic Reviews

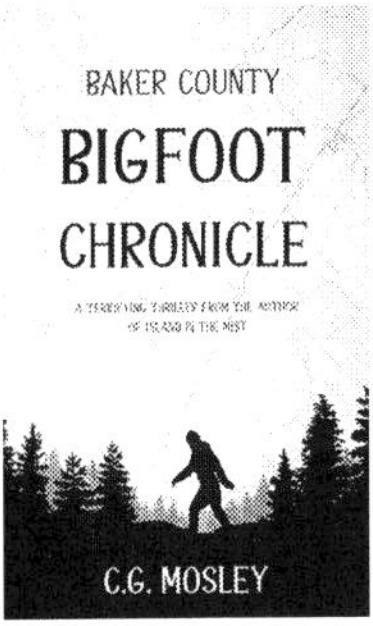

C.G. Mosley

BAKER COUNTY BIGFOOT CHRONICLE

Marie Bledsoe only wants her missing brother Kurt back. She'll stop at nothing to make it happen and, with the help of Kurt's friend Tony, along with Sheriff Ray Cochran, Marie embarks on a terrifying journey deep into the belly of the mysterious Walker Laboratory to find him. However, what she and her companions find lurking in the laboratory basement is beyond comprehension. There are cryptids from the forest being held captive there and something...else. Enjoy this suspenseful tale from the mind of C.G. Mosley, author of Wood Ape. Welcome back to Baker County, a place where monsters do lurk in the night!

SEVERED**PRESS**

@severedpress
/severedpress

Check out other great

Cryptid Novels!

Ian Faulkner

CRYPTID

Be careful what you look for. You might just find it.1996. A group of 14 students walked into the trackless virgin forests of Graham Island, British Columbia for a three-day hike. They were never seen again. 2019. An American TV crew retrace those students' steps to attempt to solve a 23-year-old mystery.A disparate collection of characters arrives on the island. But all is not as it seems. Two of them carry dark secrets. Terrible knowledge that will mean death for some – but a fighting chance of survival for others. In the hidden depths of the forests – man is on the menu. Some mysteries should remain unsolved...

Eric S. Brown

LOCH NESS HORROR

The Order of the Eternal Light, a secret organization have foretold the end of the human race. In order to save all humanity, agents of the Order must locate the Loch Ness Monster and obtain a sample of its blood for within in it is the key to stopping the apocalypse but finding the monster will be no easy task.

SEVEREDPRESS

@severedpress
/severedpress

Check out other great

Cryptid Novels!

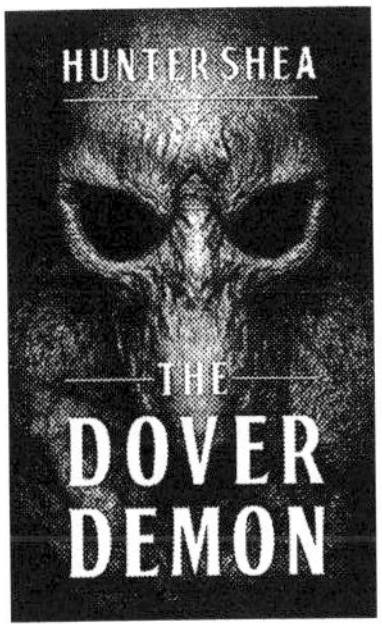

Hunter Shea

THE DOVER DEMON

The Dover Demon is real...and it has returned. In 1977, Sam Brogna and his friends came upon a terrifying, alien creature on a deserted country road. What they witnessed was so bizarre, so chilling, they swore their silence. But their lives were changed forever. Decades later, the town of Dover has been hit by a massive blizzard. Sam's son, Nicky, is drawn to search for the infamous cryptid, only to disappear into the bowels of a secret underground lair. The Dover Demon is far deadlier than anyone could have believed. And there are many of them. Can Sam and his reunited friends rescue Nicky and battle a race of creatures so powerful, so sinister, that history itself has been shaped by their secretive presence? "THE DOVER DEMON is Shea's most delightful and insidiously terrifying monster yet." – Shotgun Logic Reviews "An excellent horror novel and a strong standout in the UFO and cryptid subgenres." –Hellnotes "Non-stop action awaits those brave enough to dive into the small town of Dover, and if you're lucky, you won't see the Demon himself!" – The Scary Reviews PRAISE FOR SWAMP MONSTER MASSACRE "B-horror movie fans rejoice, Hunter Shea is here to bring you the ultimate tale of terror!" – Horror Novel Reviews "A nonstop thrill ride! I couldn't put this book down." – Cedar Hollow Horror Reviews

Armand Rosamilia

THE BEAST

The end of summer, 1986. With only a few days left until the new school year, twins Jeremy and Jack Schaffer are on very different paths. Jeremy is the geek, playing Dungeons & Dragons with friends Kathleen and Randy, while Jack is the jock, getting into trouble with his buddies. And then everything changes when neighbor Mister Higgins is killed by a wild animal in his yard. Was it a bear? There's something big lurking in the woods behind their New Jersey home.Will the police be able to solve the murder before more Middletown residents are ripped apart?

Manufactured by Amazon.ca
Bolton, ON

40061037R00085